A Belgian Assortment
BRUSSELS SHORT STORIES

T.D. ARKENBERG

outskirts
press

A Belgian Assortment
Brussels Short Stories
All Rights Reserved.
Copyright © 2019 T.D. Arkenberg
v3.0

This is a work of fiction. The events and characters described herein are imaginary and are not intended to refer to specific places or living persons. The opinions expressed in this manuscript are solely the opinions of the author and do not represent the opinions or thoughts of the publisher. The author has represented and warranted full ownership and/or legal right to publish all the materials in this book.

This book may not be reproduced, transmitted, or stored in whole or in part by any means, including graphic, electronic, or mechanical without the express written consent of the publisher except in the case of brief quotations embodied in critical articles and reviews.

Outskirts Press, Inc.
http://www.outskirtspress.com

Paperback ISBN: 978-1-9772-0253-6
Hardback ISBN: 978-1-9772-0308-3

Cover design by Susan Jackson O'Leary

Outskirts Press and the "OP" logo are trademarks belonging to Outskirts Press, Inc.

PRINTED IN THE UNITED STATES OF AMERICA

For our good friends, acquaintances, and colleagues who call Brussels home. Your kindness and camaraderie helped two American expats from Chicago survive and flourish in our adopted home.

Also by T.D. Arkenberg

Final Descent
Jell-O and Jackie O
None Shall Sleep
Two Towers

Contents

Introduction i

Chatelain Market 1
Aftershock 12
Trappistes and Trenches 24
Lockdown 38
Stuff of Dreams 51

A Belgian Photo Assortment 79

In Bruges…Again 97
Will-o'-the-Wisp 116
Parvis de Saint-Gilles 134
The Ginger Cat 146
Christmas Carousel 157
Recycled Promises 177
Marguerite and the Grand Sablon 190

Acknowledgments 207

Introduction

In January 2014, my spouse and I, along with our beloved golden retriever, moved to Brussels. Today, the centuries-old city claims 1.2 million inhabitants. Not only the capital of Belgium, Brussels also hosts NATO headquarters as well as key institutions of the European Union. As a result, the city is often called the de facto capital of Europe. Although French and Flemish are the city's official languages, English is widely spoken on account of the many expats from around the globe who call Brussels home. For two years, my spouse and I embraced the cosmopolitan metropolis and immersed ourselves in the culture of our adopted home.

Travelers capture memories in a photo album, preserve mementos in a shadow box, or detail adventures in a diary or memoir. For writers of creative fiction, seeds of truth often germinate in the mind, blossoming forth as colorful and captivating tales. I've chosen, therefore, the short story to chronicle our incredible journey. Drawn from actual observations, conversations, and personal insights, each of the tales is nonetheless fiction with characters born and developed in my imagination.

It is my hope that taken together, this collection, *A Belgian Assortment*, provides readers with a rich impression and valid representation of the modern, multi-faceted city of Brussels.

Chatelain Market

He's flirting with me, there's no mistaking it.
The thought raced through Marion's mind as she collected her change from the man selling Moroccan savories. Her knees wobbled; her heart raced. Oh, how she wanted to flirt back. But she didn't want to appear foolish, embarrass herself. She wasn't brought up that way. Instead, Marion put the five-euro note and coins in her change purse and grabbed the paper bag containing a chicken and almond pie. She was almost too flustered to respond to his velvet-toned "*Merci*," delivering a hasty "*Bon journ*èe" over her retreating shoulder.

Stupid, foolish girl, Marion thought as she pushed through walls of shoppers who lined up in front of the fishmonger's truck and another stall whose purveyor served up steamed mussels, boiled shrimp, and croquettes. Marion had taken weeks to muster the courage to buy the Moroccan savory, a puff pastry of sorts the size and shape of a pincushion. Feeling her face warm, she fought the urge to get angry with herself. *It's okay. Next time, I'll be ready. Just have to prepare my response, that's all.*

Marion came to the market at Chatelain every week after her shift in a shop inside the Galeries Saint-Hubert. On Wednesday afternoons, vendors in caravans, tents, covered stalls, and large specialty trucks transformed an otherwise drab and unremarkable car park into a vibrant street party complete with food and drink. There were the customary market offerings of fruit, vegetables, meats, fish, baguettes, and cheeses. And similar to the vendors at the city's many morning markets, peddlers offered tubs of colorful, fragrant flowers for sale at reasonable prices. Chatelain, however, offered an additional enticement—an exotic buffet of nose-teasing, mouth-watering delicacies.

Those who strolled under canvas marquees might happen upon sweet and savory crepes, quiche, olive tapenades and hummus, roasted chicken, meat pies, Portuguese sweet tarts, pad Thai, egg rolls, panini, African stews, shrimp and lobster bisques, mussels and oysters. Friends, couples, and work colleagues sat at portable café tables in tents and under trees drinking beer or sipping wine and champagne from glassware while nibbling the cuisine of their choice. Pleasant chatter and laughter filled the air.

Assuming a carnival atmosphere, the afternoon market at Chatelain was a feast for the eyes, ears, nose, and palate. Only the fiercest of rainstorms kept Marion away. In addition to local residents of the chic district, the market drew expats and professionals who worked in and around Avenue Louise, the European Union quarter, and even downtown. Sleek electric trams carried commuters and market-goers along Avenue Louise and Rue du Bailli. Marion usually traveled to the market from the central city via public transport. It was the one evening a week that she didn't mind crowding into the oppressive tram car, being jostled by strange men, and having to listen to the mindless banter of uppity women in business suits and flashy attire.

Marion relished the evenings of late spring and summer. With the sun high in the sky at six and even seven o'clock, she pretended she was a lady of leisure enjoying a free afternoon instead of a shop clerk whose feet ached from eight hours of standing behind a candy counter. Upon arriving at the market, Marion kept to a routine, strolling the stalls and caravans first clockwise and then counterclockwise.

In addition to an occasional purchase of produce, cheese, and flowers, Marion stole glances at handsome men. Her recent fascination was the vendor who sold Moroccan food items. Tall and trim, he had features that were a mix of the exotic and familiar: olive skin, dark eyes, a prominent nose, and thick short hair, more brown than black. Despite Marion's best efforts, she hadn't yet learned his name. For all she knew, his closest encounter with Morocco was a North African cookbook. Still, Marion tagged her latest crush "the Moroccan."

Every week, as Marion paused to sip wine purchased from one of the market stalls that dispensed alcohol, she dabbled in fantasy. There was the beefy hulk of a man with tattoos who sold Portuguese custard tarts. A wavy-haired hunk with thick eyebrows and massive biceps peddled Italian coffee. The Moroccan was merely her latest obsession. She considered the possibility that he was the product of a passionate fling between a Belgian woman and a North African man, or vice versa. Perhaps he was born during the height of the Algerian conflict, his parents fleeing across the Mediterranean to France. *No,* she reasoned in her head, *he's younger than that. Just a few years older than me. Nearer forty than fifty.* Maybe he was ex-military or sought the casual market life to escape a shady past. A jewel thief or better yet, gigolo. *God knows he has the looks and personality to charm his way into a woman's heart and bed.*

Marion observed that she wasn't alone in her admiration. Young women flocked to the man's food stand. A perfect smile, playful teasing, and a physique that fit nicely into worn jeans made the Moroccan a natural at peddling his exotic offerings. Many of his female customers, however, were bolder than Marion. Despite a gold wedding band and the occasional appearance of a pretty but aloof woman who shared the booth, the Moroccan inspired flirtatious banter. The most brazen of these flirtations made Marion blush.

Marion wanted to believe the Moroccan's snooty associate with light-brown skin and long dark hair was his sister. Marion discounted the pair's affectionate greetings. Other shoppers, she assumed, felt the same. The woman's presence didn't deter fawning female fans or stifle the man's flirtations. Apparently the couple, whatever their relationship, accepted the fact that sex sold Moroccan meat pies.

What I wouldn't give to trade my job selling chocolates to work beside the Moroccan. That desire had replayed itself in Marion's head in recent weeks as she toured the market. But it wasn't her first romantic fantasy inspired by Chatelain. In the past, Marion had imagined quitting her job to work in a variety of market stalls, always beside a strong, handsome man.

Placing the food sack with a growing grease stain onto an empty table, Marion got in line to order a glass of wine. In front of her stood an older gentleman and his poodle. At first glance, the man cut a fine, distinguished figure. He wore a crisply pressed shirt, tailored blue blazer, and creased gray trousers. But when the sun broke through the clouds, Marion noticed the tattered reality. The man's trousers were shiny, the cuffs worn; his shirt collar frayed, and the blazer was stained. Despite a polished sheen, the man's shoes showed signs of wear. Marion stifled a giggle as she considered the likeness between the poodle and its owner: white untamed hair, round eyes set close together, and a small pointed nose.

After waiting for the white-haired man to measure out exact change for his purchase in small coins, Marion paid her two euros, fifty for a glass of Chardonnay. The mother and son who ran the stall didn't serve up the best wine at the market, but theirs was the cheapest.

The wine vendor's jumble of short metal tables and stools also held a strategic advantage. In addition to a towering oak that provided shade as well as protection from light drizzle, the stall's location facilitated Marion's dabbles into fantasy. Sitting at one of the small red tables, Marion could nurse one, maybe two drinks for an hour, watching the parade of people. Even better, she could stare furtively at the Moroccan.

Other patrons often seized the empty stools from Marion's side without comment, removing them to join comrades partying elsewhere. On occasion, strangers asked to join her. The more polite of those who did so, usually tourists, engaged Marion in conversation. Most, however, turned their backs to Marion, using her table merely as a perch for glasses, food, and trash. Marion didn't mind being left alone.

She preferred it. All at once, she was part of the carnival atmosphere, yet apart—a spectator with a ringside seat.

After Marion bit into the Moroccan savory, she recalled why she didn't make a habit of eating it. She didn't really care for the meat pies. As she washed away the bitter aftertaste of almonds and pungent spices with cheap wine, Marion eavesdropped on two young women chatting at another table. She recognized them from the Moroccan's stand. They made a huge, and in Marion's opinion, overly dramatic fuss over his gold bracelet. *One actually pawed his arm, for God's sake.* Despite envying their confidence and the ease with which they bantered with the charming vendor, Marion decided that she didn't like the pair. They were too cutesy, forward, and shameless, the kind of silly girls that her aunt, Agnes Marie, called harlots. *Besides, they were rude to monopolize the Moroccan's attention while I waited to place my order.*

Marion assumed that the blonde was a visitor on holiday. She guessed that the other woman, a brunette wearing a yellow sleeveless dress, worked for the European Union. In the two decades she'd lived in Brussels and worked in retail, Marion recognized the legions of foreigners who belonged to the *Corps Diplomatique.*

"Did you get his name?" the blonde asked the other, her accent American. The woman's long silky hair, a shade or two lighter than Marion's, fell below her shoulders. She wore denim shorts and a pink floral blouse over a white camisole. Her toenails were painted bright pink, a contrast to her white sandals. The woman's silver ankle bracelet drew Marion's scowl.

"I think it's Jean-Marc. Or maybe just plain Marc," replied her friend. Marion placed the accent as Scandinavian. The perky brunette wore her hair short. It was an expensive cut that swept her bangs off her forehead. Her dress and appearance were professional and quite stylish. "But it's not his name that interests me," the brunette added.

The blonde laughed. "Great eyes, lips—"

"And?" the other woman interrupted her friend with lifted eyebrow and suggestive tone.

"OMG. When he bent over the cash box to make us change," the American said with a sigh. "If I lived in Brussels, Eva, I'd be here every week…asking for change." She bit into a meat pie and grimaced. "Nice butt, but his pies are dreadful."

Eva laughed. "It's settled then. Jean-Marc's all mine," she said pulling the remainder of her friend's savory toward her. "I looove his *meat…pies.*"

Rolling her eyes, Marion thought the blonde, quaking with laughter, would squirt wine through her nose. Marion winced. The image again recalled Agnes Marie, the stern aunt who had raised Marion in Liège after her parents were killed in a car accident.

Marion had just turned twelve. She and her younger cousin Caroline, the aunt's daughter, were sitting at the kitchen table. Marion confided in Caroline about her crush on a cute new classmate. The Jordanian boy had just immigrated to Belgium. Marion fantasized about his kissing her. When she mentioned his name, Ali Walii, Caroline squirted milk through her nose.

"Marion's got a boyfriend, Marion's got a boyfriend." Caroline chanted the words like a toddler. "Olly Wolly, Olly Wolly. Jolly, Olly Wolly. K-i-s-s-i-n-g."

"Shut up! He's not my boyfriend." Marion felt heat in her face.

She didn't see it coming. The sound was louder than she could have imagined. The force knocked her off the chair and onto the hard linoleum floor. Stunned and dazed, Marion's hand flew to her stinging cheek. Aunt Agnes stood over her, fire in her eyes. Marion's gaze wandered to the wall behind her aunt. The hand-painted porcelain Jesus looked down from the cross, its aqua-blue eyes also glaring at her in judgment.

"No niece of mine is going to be a harlot. Not while you're under my roof. You're too young for boys. And by the grace of our Virgin Mother, *never* with a heathen. Do you hear me?"

Only then did Marion start to sob. Lifting herself off the floor, she ran from the room. Falling onto her bed, she cried herself to sleep.

But the ordeal wasn't over. Aunt Agnes dragged her to confession, advising the priest in a loud voice, which turned heads, that her niece had impure thoughts. Marion had never been more embarrassed or ashamed.

Later, when other girls her age started wearing makeup, Marion didn't dare. Instead of rebelling, she withdrew into herself. She spent nights in her bedroom listening to Christian music and reading paperback romances she snuck into the house.

Marion's entry into womanhood wasn't easy. Her first period horrified her. *Is it God's revenge? Will I die and go to hell?* Her sheltered mind even paused to wonder whether the steamy romance novels might have brought on the never-before-experienced condition. She was terrified that Aunt Agnes would find out and label her a harlot or slut. Marion suffered in silence, learning about puberty only from other girls at school.

Marion couldn't wait to leave her aunt's house, escaping Liège when she turned eighteen. She hadn't been in Brussels even a year when she learned of her cousin's news. She felt sorry for Caroline. Her cousin was ill-prepared to be a single mother at fifteen. Marion's sympathy, however, didn't extend to Aunt Agnes.

"Excuse me, my dear. My dear…"

The voice drew Marion's mind back to Chatelain. She felt a presence as her eyes focused on the white dog at her feet. "Oh, pardon, pardon." Looking up, she found the white-haired man she had noticed in line for wine counting out his coins. "Must have been daydreaming."

He smiled; his blue eyes twinkled with kindness. "No worries, dear girl. Heat and wine do that to the best of us. May I sit, or are you expecting someone?"

"Sit, sit, please," Marion replied, pushing together her wineglass and meat pie although the table had plenty of space.

The man introduced himself as Armande, and Marion reciprocated in giving her name. After placing a fresh glass of wine on the table, the older man removed a bouquet of pink peonies from beneath his arm. He placed them next to his glass.

Marion gasped. "Oh no!" Her cry was loud enough for others, including the blonde and brunette women, to turn toward her. The attention flustered her. She felt dizzy, light-headed.

Concern swept across Armande's face. "What is it, dear girl? Are you okay?"

Marion rose to her feet, her eyes darting toward the Moroccan's stall. She gasped for air. "My flowers. Left them…at the…food…. Peonies…just like yours."

Marion turned down Armande's offer of help, asking him merely to watch her things. Moments later she returned, her chin down, her expression somber. Armande was still seated at her table with his dog.

"Didn't find your flowers, dear girl?"

Marion sighed. "Yes and no." She explained that the peony bouquet was no longer on the counter of the food stall where she had left it. The Moroccan claimed not to have seen her flowers. "'Someone must have taken them,' he said. 'Market's full of shady characters,' he said. 'Beautiful woman like you needs to be extra careful.'"

"Very sorry," Armande said, shaking his head. "But you said, 'Yes and no.' What does that mean?"

"Never mind." Marion was too upset and embarrassed. How could she tell him that she saw the Moroccan's wife, for assuredly she was his wife, walk away from the stall, a purse in one hand, and Marion's peony bouquet in the other?

"He offered me one of those awful pies.…" she mumbled more to herself than to Armande. If Marion weren't so angry, she'd have cried. "I should go."

"Nonsense, dear girl. Shame about your flowers, but don't let that spoil your afternoon. Sun won't set till ten o'clock. You still have plenty of wine left. And see," he added, pointing to Marion's feet. "Oliver wants you to stay. He's a jolly fellow."

Marion looked toward the ground. The white poodle had wound

its leash around her ankle. The dog looked up at her. She smiled. Oliver was cute and, yes, jolly, if not a bit rumpled for a poodle. After they untangled the leash, Marion sat down. Petting the dog calmed her.

"I'd let you have my flowers, but they're for my wife," Armande said somewhat apologetically, or so Marion thought. "Peonies are her favorite." Marion noticed the look of deep affection on the man's face.

"Mine too."

Armande shook his head. "End of the season, I'm afraid. There won't be any next week."

Marion nodded, her thoughts briefly wandering to her lost flowers and wilted fantasy.

Sipping wine, Armande and Marion talked about the market. It was a safe topic for two strangers. Marion didn't want to bore him with her shallow life, and she figured he was too old-fashioned to share private information. Armande, she learned, had only started coming to Chatelain in recent weeks. The market was his wife's favorite. Marion guessed that he was recently retired or his wife wanted a break from the weekly shopping. Either way, Marion was glad for the company.

Armande stood up. "Will you excuse me? Could you watch Oliver?"

Marion nodded as she reached for the leash. She assumed Armande had to use the toilet. As she waited, several people paused to look at the dog. An English couple stopped to pet him. Marion loved the attention, the most she had ever attracted at Chatelain.

"Is this seat free?"

Marion turned toward the deep voice. A ruggedly handsome man had stooped to pet Oliver. He motioned to Armande's vacant seat, repeating his question. Marion stammered. She wanted to say yes. *Can I do that to Armande? I don't owe the old man anything.*

Struggling with her decision, she replied that the seat was occupied. So, instead of sharing her spot, Marion watched as the sexy young man took his beer over to the next table. The two giddy flirts gladly shared their table and giggles with the man.

Marion scratched the dog behind the ears. "Just isn't my day, Oliver."

Armande returned with a bouquet of flowers, a colorful mix of roses and purple statice. Marion felt terrible. The poor old guy had counted out his wine money in coins. She didn't mean for him to buy her flowers.

"All out of peonies, dear girl. Just as I feared."

"Armande, you shouldn't have."

"I didn't."

"So s…stupid of me. I…I just assumed they were—"

He laughed. "There, there, my dear. The roses are for my wife," he said, holding up the new bouquet. "You may have the peonies." He pushed the bouquet toward her. "With Oliver's and my compliments."

"You mustn't. What about your wife?"

Armande's eyes twinkled. He seemed younger than her first impression. "Edita won't mind. You'll get much more joy out of the peonies than she will."

"You can't mean that. You said they're her favorite."

His lips formed a mischievous smile. He was more handsome than she first thought. "She won't even know. You see, the flowers…well… they're for her grave." He responded to Marion's flinch of surprise by squeezing her hand. "It's okay. I've got to learn to let go. My wife made me promise as much. You see, we knew she was going to die for some time. Coming to Chatelain is my way of being with her while rejoining the world."

Over another glass of wine, Marion and Armande shared stories of favorite films, books, and music. Marion was surprised to learn how much they had in common. They were so absorbed in conversation that they didn't notice the market start to shut down. Only when the wine vendor came to reclaim his table did they realize the time. They bade each other farewell.

"Ollie and I will be here next Wednesday. Will you, dear Marion?"

Marion grinned. She gave the tail-wagging poodle a scratch

behind the ears before leaning forward and kissing her new friend's cheek. "If you and Jolly Ollie come, so will I." She glanced toward the Moroccan's shuttered stall. "But let's try the wine and food on the other side of Chatelain Market."

Aftershock

"War destroyed the Grand Place but saved the Town Hall." The blaring sound of the dismissal bell prevented Sabine from further explanation.

Damn! she thought as her pupils bolted for the door. The Bombardment of Brussels couldn't compete with a sunny, late September afternoon. She'd have to clarify her meaning at the beginning of the next session or risk leaving students with the impression that Louis XIV's artillery had destroyed Brussels in the name of building preservation.

Sabine hated the days when she couldn't get through her lesson plan. Instead of a full, vibrant picture she strove so hard to draw, she left her students with mere fragments of history. With increasing frequency, disciplinary matters stole her instruction time. Even when she didn't have her hands full refereeing arguments between pupils, she found her authority questioned or worse, dismissed by eleven- and twelve-year-old boys. They didn't always verbalize their prejudices, but the rage that flashed in their eyes was unmistakable.

It had been three months, one of the last days of the prior school year, since a rather painful outburst. The boy, baby-faced Mehdi, had embarrassed her in front of the entire class. "What makes you think you can teach?" he shouted after she corrected his claim that Belgium would never have a queen. "You're just a stupid woman."

Sabine tried to push the words from her mind. She had the entire summer to bolster her self-confidence. Two weeks on the Belgian coast in August helped, despite gray skies, crowded sidewalks, and overpriced meals. Erik had been a real sweetheart too, letting her sleep late and offering light massages as she lay on a chaise longue on the beach. She should have figured that things were going too well. He became argumentative late in their holiday, during an afternoon of too much beer and self-pity over returning to an overbearing boss and a dead-end job. She'd grown used to Erik's increasing sullenness, but his verbal abuse was something new.

Sabine began her fourth year at Sint Albert, a primary school that offered instruction in Flemish, flirting with her own frustrations. She mentally readied herself for the new year with a vow not to let *the little darlings*, as she called them, get under her skin. She owed it to the good kids, the ones who wanted to learn. And there were plenty of them. If only their voices drowned out the bullies. *Merely childish rhetoric*, she repeated in her head. *Could happen anywhere*. If only she believed that. She was sinking into a deep despair, a feeling of profound isolation, not only at school but also in her adopted city and, to be honest, even at home with Erik.

Sabine was born and educated in Ghent. Her parents weren't happy when she decided to move to Brussels. "It's dirty, unsafe," they said. "And to think it was once a Flemish city." Her mom and dad were good people, but even they had their prejudices. Simple, working-class people, they didn't venture beyond their close circle of family and friends, mostly white, Catholic, and proudly Flemish. Her parents' small world was immune to the demographic changes taking place across Belgium. They didn't object to the social evolution; they simply didn't want any part of it. Sabine wasn't interested in that kind of life. A university degree had exposed her to sophistication and diversity.

"If you must take that job, why don't you commute?" That was her mother's last-ditch effort to keep her daughter anchored in Flanders.

Sabine didn't want to waste her life sitting in Belgian traffic.

Strong bonds that kept people tethered to families and childhood friends were often given as explanations for the country's notoriously long commutes and clogged motorways. Perhaps traffic was merely a convenient excuse. In truth, Sabine wanted to escape her clan.

Sabine was determined. Her partner Erik, a boy she had known since primary school, snared an entry-level position with the European Commission. "Play my cards right, avoid a murder conviction or drug-smuggling charge," Erik said with a laugh, "and it's a job for life."

The couple found a cheap but adequate flat just off Place Sainte-Catherine, an area popular with young professionals and tourists. Sabine and Erik embraced the carnival atmosphere that descended upon the square on weekends. They dismissed the smattering of vagrants and drunks, drawn by the abundance of bars and cafés, as mere urban color.

The church that gave the square its name never failed to impress Sabine. At night, bathed in spotlight, its magnificent stone edifice radiated with an orange-apricot glow reminiscent of the setting sun. During their first year or so, Erik and Sabine used to sit on a park bench holding hands, taking in their exciting neighborhood, and sharing news of their days. In recent months, however, Sabine sought solitary refuge on the bench away from Erik and the simmering stresses of home.

Sabine's parents were right on one account. Despite the daily rounds of street sweepers, Brussels never cleaned up very well. Rubbish littered the gutters while animal waste, missing paving stones, and beggars turned the narrow sidewalks into obstacle courses. After too many sneers and "told you so" remarks, Sabine stopped inviting her parents for weekend visits.

As for language, at first Sabine found the predominance of French speakers quaint, even a bit exotic. But as time passed and frustrations with her job and life mounted, she grew aggravated that most shopkeepers and others she met on the street didn't speak or even understand Flemish. "I'm a stranger in my own country," she complained. "It's *my* capital too, damn it."

With her mind focused on the interrupted lesson of the 1695 Bombardment of Brussels, Sabine hustled down the gray corridor toward the teachers' lounge. Except for a friendly Congolese janitor and a couple of teacher's aides chatting in front of an open classroom, the hall was deserted. The hour after classes let out for the afternoon had become her favorite part of the workday. She worried that she was losing her passion. *Am I turning into one of those jaded teachers I swore I'd never become?*

"Hello, Sabine," said Hilde, a tall, slender woman with gray hair pulled back into a bun. The veteran teacher never used makeup. She wore her creases and weathered skin as a badge of honor. "Teachers' faces are like tree rings. Every year brings another wrinkle. You'll see." Hilde had provided that counsel to a fresh-faced Sabine on her first day at Sint Albert. As part of an informal mentoring program designed to discourage new teachers from quitting, Hilde took Sabine under her wing. "Haven't put in your notice today, my dear, have you?"

"Not yet, but the day's not over," Sabine said with a short laugh.

The exchange had become an after-school ritual, a running joke between the two friends. But this afternoon, Sabine's canned retort had merit. Her day wasn't over. She had one more appointment, a parent conference concerning one of her more persistent rabble-rousers.

Sabine sat at one of the large metal tables in the lounge. Teachers returned from summer holidays to find their break room painted bright yellow with a border of daisies where the walls met the ceiling. Pastel-colored mugs replaced black, chipped cups. "Some of the little things we can do to lift morale," the principal, Mr. Mickelsen, said in remarks welcoming teachers back to school. But all the new paint and colorful china couldn't camouflage the shabbiness of the building, a postwar eyesore of steel, beige brick and grimy glass.

Hilde placed two mugs, pink and robin's-egg blue, on the table and took a seat across from the younger woman.

"Rough day?" Hilde asked, blowing on the steaming tea.

Sabine poured milk into her mug without looking at the other woman. "I'll say. Seems I spend more time keeping peace than teaching. Still don't understand why they can't get along."

"It's cultural. The little monsters hate each other, that's why."

"You talking about my people?"

Sabine and Hilde turned toward the deep voice. Youssef, the new mathematics instructor, stood in the doorway. Sabine blushed. She thought the tall man, about her age or a bit older, maybe even thirty, was very handsome. Dark eyes, hair, and skin couldn't have been more different from her fair Flemish features or those of her partner Erik. The snug white polo shirt Youssef wore accentuated his exotic features and muscular frame.

"Oh…oh, sorry. W…we d…didn't mean to offend—" Sabine stammered.

Hilde threw her a scowl. "Sorry? For telling the truth? Pish posh!"

Sabine had a sense that Hilde didn't like Youssef, but it was too early in the term to tell. Proclaiming herself a "crusty old lesbian," Hilde proudly passed judgment on newcomers to the teaching staff. "They accept me, I accept them. Simple as that," she explained. "Like? Well, that's a different matter altogether."

Youssef laughed. The flash of his brilliant white teeth contrasted with the dark stubble of his neatly trimmed beard. Sabine hadn't noticed before how full his lips were. "No offense taken," he said. "In these skirmishes, I'm on your side. Same at my last school. They can be little bastards. Love to pummel them myself if they wouldn't bruise."

Sabine's blue eyes grew wide; she looked to the door then back to Youssef, avoiding direct eye contact. "Shh. Mustn't say things like that. Mr. Mickelsen doesn't approve."

Hilde rolled her eyes at her young protégée. "The truth hurts, Miss Three-Wrinkles. You'll learn that soon enough," she said, tracing a deep line that creased her cheek from nose to chin. Hilde looked up at Youssef and pulled a chair out from the table. "Care to join us?"

"Sure. Got time for a quick cup before boys' basketball." Youssef walked toward the electric kettle and poured the still-hot water into a glass containing a tea bag.

Sabine returned her gaze from the male teacher's athletic backside to find Hilde, her eyebrows lifted, grinning at her. After Sabine had confided in Hilde about troubles with Erik, the older woman took up the mantle of matchmaker. Batting her hand at the other woman, Sabine felt embarrassed and worse, foolish. Youssef wasn't her type, at least she didn't think so. Her parents wouldn't approve, not that she cared. Or did she? It wasn't prejudice. She simply had always imagined herself settling down with a solid Flemish boy like Erik.

"It'd make all of our lives much easier if you could convince your… *people* to get along," Hilde said to Youssef when he joined the two women at the table.

"They don't listen to me any more than they do you."

Hilde cleared her throat. "Ahem, you are a man."

Youssef nodded. "True. But even that doesn't make a difference in the struggle between Turks and Moroccans."

"What are you?" Sabine said, instantly regretting her forwardness. "Oh, so sorry. You don't have to answer that. Forget I asked." She felt her cheeks warm.

He smiled; his eyes crinkled at the corners. "Let's see. I'm a football fanatic who's addicted to hamburgers, *pommes frites,* and Chimay Bleu. I'm a jazz lover, a cat owner, a Scorpio…and, yes, a Belgian of Moroccan descent."

"Scorpio, huh?" Hilde said. "Got the looks for it. That's for sure." She winked at Youssef. "Now you're both blushing. That's good. No one's at a disadvantage."

Youssef regained his composure. "Don't mind you asking. Both of my grandfathers immigrated in the sixties, from the same village. Worked the coal mines. My parents were born in Charleroi. And, yes, before you ask, theirs was an arranged marriage."

"But you're single?" Hilde asked, not even trying to conceal her mischievous grin.

Youssef nodded. "No prospects, I'm afraid. Can't impress the ladies on a teacher's salary."

Sabine glanced up at the clock shaped like a full-rayed sun, a new addition to the room. "Oh, my. Must run. Parent conference for one of my little…darlings."

"What's for dinner?"

Sabine shook her head. She hadn't even extracted the key from the lock of the flat's front door. "And a *good evening* to you too, darling Erik." She shut the door and placed the plastic grocery bags from Carrefour onto the kitchen table. "How about leeks and carrots? I've been mending too many popped buttons." *He deserves the jab about his ballooning weight,* she thought.

"Very funny." Erik came up behind her and kissed the nape of her neck. "I'm sorry, honey. How was your day?"

"Chicken, green beans, and potatoes." Her voice was cold, monotone.

"Huh? Oh, come on. I said I was sorry."

Keeping her back to him, Sabine merely shrugged.

"Tell me. I'm interested, really, I am."

Sabine dropped a bag of potatoes on the table with a thud and turned toward Erik. "Horrible. It's only week three and I'm ready to surrender. The kids are out of control. Parents aren't much better."

Erik squeezed her shoulders. "Sit. Let me pour you some wine."

"What about din—"

"Relax. Dinner can wait."

Erik helped Sabine out of her light-blue raincoat. He guided her to a soft chair in the living room. She heard the dull pop of a cork and the clanking of glass before he returned with a tumbler of white wine. He sat on the sofa opposite her and lifted a blue can of beer off the side table. From the stale smell of his breath and the glassy stare, Sabine knew it wasn't his first.

Gazing at his face, she pictured him with a beard. "Ever try Chimay Bleu?"

A puzzled look flashed across Erik's clean-shaven face and was gone in an instant. "Too expensive, bitter. Now, tell me about your day."

Sabine described her frustrations with the parent conference. It was always the same story: mothers who came alone, fathers who couldn't be bothered.

"At least Hamed's mother was honest. She earns points there."

Erik sat forward. "What did she say?"

"'Hamed's father thinks the boy would do better with a male teacher,' she said. Can you imagine? That's where the kids get this shit."

"Sorry, honey. That's all fucked up. I wish you didn't work there."

"But I do. Can't quit." She looked into Erik's eyes, red and puffy from too much alcohol. "May as well get used to it."

Erik wriggled back into the cushions; he dropped his chin. "Guess this is the wrong time to bring up our freaky neighbors."

Sabine rolled her eyes toward the ceiling before reclining her head. She offered a sigh of surrender. She'd grown tired of Erik's wild stories. He'd become convinced that the two brothers, Middle Eastern by language and appearance, were terrorists. Sabine dismissed his suspicions as xenophobia, too much beer, and an overactive imagination.

She forbade him to share his suspicions with her parents. "That's all they need." She imagined being dragged back to Ghent by her hysterical mother and judgmental father. So far, Sabine had managed to keep Erik from calling the police. Work and Erik's increased drinking and mood swings were stressful enough. She didn't want to introduce even more strife into her life by waging war with the neighbors.

"I'm serious, honey. Don't you want to hear what I saw today?"

Sabine sat up and groaned. After taking a large gulp of wine, she glared across at her partner. She had no time for this nonsense. "No! I'm sorry, but I have to deal with these people every day while you traipse off to the EU. The least you can do is put up with a little neighborly irritation. This is Brussels, for God's sake. May as well get used to it."

Checking herself out in the bedroom mirror, Sabine was pleased with her reflection. She looked radiant for the final day of the school year and her very last day at Sint Albert. To a new black dress with white blazer from Zara and her blonde hair done up in a short chic summer cut she added the silver and lapis earrings and matching pendant for good luck. They were a Valentine's Day gift—from Youssef.

Have the last nine months been a dream? Her life had undergone a stunning transformation. Besides exchanging Erik for Youssef, she landed a job at the prestigious International School in Boitsfort beginning later that fall. She and Youssef agreed that he'd continue at Sint Albert until she established herself at the new school. He was in no rush to leave Sint Albert anyway. He was encouraged. His afternoon basketball program had bridged the cultural divide between the feuding factions of boys. She and Youssef planned to use the summer break to find a flat on the nicer side of town: Ixelles, Uccle, or maybe even nearer her new job in Boitsfort.

Sabine leaned closer to the mirror. Studying her face, she grinned. There it was, wrinkle number four—her badge of honor. She'd proudly point it out to Hilde who'd begin calling her Miss Four-Wrinkles.

Sabine practically floated toward the tram stop in her new shoes. It was a beautiful June morning, even by Brussels standards. Looking to the horizon, she grinned at the memory of her interrupted lesson at the beginning of the school year. Atop the Town Hall, the gilt statue of Michael the Archangel, the city's patron saint, gleamed in the morning sun.

At the sight of the school building, Sabine's stomach knotted. *Mix of excitement and goodbye jitters, that's all,* she thought. An idling lawnmower sat unattended in the building's small front garden. *Careless,* she thought, as she mounted the stone steps to the entrance. *And with small children expected within the half hour.* Inside, she glanced toward the Administration Office opposite the front door. *Perhaps I should report the lawnmower?* But Mr. Mickelsen's vigilant secretary wasn't at her post. The spinster with a permanent frown usually perched at her desk like an old barn owl, keeping tabs on the comings of staff.

Things seemed odd, upended. The two corridors leading from the front vestibule were deserted. Normally, a few teachers shuttled between classrooms. Even Mr. Finch, a steadfast creature of habit with whom Sabine exchanged a daily morning greeting, wasn't at his desk eating crackers and reading *The Times of London.*

"This isn't the weekend or a holiday?" she muttered to herself. *No, the doors would be locked.* There was also the idling lawnmower.

She gasped. *That's it!* Sabine guessed that the school staff was gathered in the lounge. *A surprise!* Her co-workers intended to surprise her on her last day. They'd send her forth from Sint Albert with farewell wishes and cake. *Hadn't Youssef hinted as much the prior night?* With a mischievous smile, and saying he had "things to do," he had left right after dinner and spent the night at his flat.

Sabine hastened her step until she approached the teachers' lounge. Hushed voices floated out the open door into the corridor. Her ears perked; her feet froze. *Are those sobs?* When she entered the doorway, her eyes took in the colorful streamers and balloons. A sheet cake with *Congratulations, Sabine* sat in the middle of the table around which Hilde and others huddled.

Hilde looked up. Instead of returning Sabine's broad grin, the older woman appeared frightened, sad—her face ashen. Rising from her chair, Hilde took Sabine's hand. "You haven't heard, have you, my dear?"

Sabine felt all eyes turn to her. "Heard what?"

"There's been an explosion—in the Metro."

"Damn terrorists again," someone else muttered.

Sabine's heart sank for the innocents. For surely there were victims. Madmen always unleashed their fury to maximize carnage. "Oh my God, no. Where?"

"Louiza."

Sabine was shocked but not surprised. Louiza was an ideal target. It was the Metro station below Tiffany, Dior, Versace, and dozens of other luxury boutiques that lined the Gulden-Vlieslaan and Louizalaan.

Hilde pulled Sabine into a firm embrace. "There's more, my dear girl." Over Hilde's shoulder, Sabine noticed Fredrik. The slight, rodent-faced science teacher looked ill, his face white. He could barely steady the coffee mug in his shaking hands. Sabine drew back and looked at Hilde. The older woman's eyes welled with tears. "I'm so sorry," she said, "so very sorry."

"Tell me, Hilde. What's happened?"

Sobs intensified among the other teachers and staff in the lounge. Sabine didn't remember much else or how she got back home.

Later that night, Sabine was alone in her flat. She wanted—no, needed—the solitude. Hilde and Mr. Mickelsen had left only after she insisted that they go home to get some rest. Sabine pleaded with her parents to drive back to Ghent without her. They were obstinate, relenting only after she agreed to consider moving back to Ghent even if only for the summer.

Clutching to her heaving chest the pendant that Youssef had given her, Sabine curled up on the couch and sobbed. The day's events kept invading her thoughts. Was it her imagination, or did she already know what happened before Hilde quelled her sobs to share the news?

Youssef had been killed. Although authorities weren't releasing any names, there was no doubt. Fredrik's account confirmed as much. He and Youssef had ridden the Metro together, bumping into each other at Kunst-Wet, three Metro stops before Louiza.

"Youssef was so excited about your last day," Fredrik told her between stammering apologies. "He couldn't stop grinning. He'd bought a gift but forgot flowers. He remembered the florist inside the Louiza station. 'I'll hop off,' Youssef said. 'Buy the biggest bouquet of roses and jump onto the next train.'"

The next Metro never left the platform. Two brothers, suicide bombers, blew up the train and the entire station.

Trappistes and Trenches

"Damn, damn, damn!"

With a look of concern on his face, Luisa Hood's husband George entered the large master bath wearing only boxer shorts. "What happened?"

Luisa stared down into the white porcelain commode. A trickle of amber liquid escaped the crystal bottle resting at the bottom. "Dropped my perfume down the blasted toilet," she replied, running her fingers through her long auburn hair.

"Let me see." Fighting an urge to laugh, George patted his wife's behind, letting his hand rest on her satin panties. "You don't need perfume to smell wonderful," he said, nuzzling her neck. She bristled, prompting him to add, "Would you like me to—"

"If only you hadn't rushed me. That's very expensive perfume. What a terrible waste." She sighed, her tone more plaintive than angry.

"Honey, I only said that I'd like to get to the airport before my brother made it through customs. Don't want to give him another reason to resent me." After kissing her cheek, George fished out the bottle. He shook the excess water into the toilet. "Looks fine to me," he added, holding it up to the light. "Now it's authentic *eau de toilette*."

Luisa chuckled. "You're right."

"I always am. But on the off chance I'm not, we get another bottle. It's only money." After setting the bottle on the marble sink, George gave her bottom a gentle pinch.

Luisa was a native of Flanders. She had married George Hood, a native of Washington DC, three years earlier. A widow for several years, she hadn't expected love to pop into her life again. But then again, she never expected to meet a tall, handsome, and very successful American. His wavy-brown hair, kind smile, and broad shoulders were extra attractions, beyond a sharp wit and charismatic personality. His employer, a large U.S. defense contractor, transferred him to Brussels as the company's chief liaison with NATO. Reluctantly, Luisa quit her job to focus on setting up the couple's spacious penthouse apartment in Ixelles as well as hosting the many social gatherings her husband's position demanded.

Luisa's fingers quivered as she replaced the bottle's topper. "What if your brother doesn't like me?"

George caressed her arm. "Are you joking? William will love you. He has to. It's his job."

Luisa pulled away. "Small comfort. I'd like to think your brother would like me for…for who I am."

George laughed. "He'll love every bit of you. Your charms, beauty, grace, wit, not to mention your earlobes, neck, shoulders…" He stopped talking to kiss the inventoried body parts.

Luisa surrendered. "I do hope so. It's just that…from what you've said…about him and your ex-wife, I mean, I worry he may not view me in a kindly light."

"Honey, I've told you. Kay and I were through long before I met you. Your only role was helping me see how I made the right decision."

"That's what I'm talking about. He may not approve…of that kind of help."

William was George's older brother. He and George's ex-wife Kay were chummy long before Kay and George married. The pair had a history of some sort, but Luisa was cloudy on the details. She never asked too many questions. She didn't want to give George the idea that she was nosy or worse, jealous of his ex-wife. Kay was never a part of their lives. Luisa was grateful to her husband for keeping it that way.

But she knew that William and Kay's continued friendship after the divorce was a source of friction between the brothers.

George embraced Luisa from behind. They stared at each other in the mirror. "Neither of them can blame you."

"B…but, it still nags me we never confessed—"

"That's *our* secret." The intensity of his tone informed her that George had no intent of sharing that piece of their history with his brother. "I moved out of the house months before my transfer to Belgium. That's all anyone needs to know. You weren't the cause of my divorce. But you are the source of my happiness. Understood?" His dark-brown eyes fixed on her until she complied with a nod. "Thatta girl. Now make yourself even more beautiful while I finish getting dressed. Besides," George added from the bedroom, "if William dislikes anyone, it's me. Oh, yes. We probably should get used to calling him *Brother* William."

George didn't talk much about his brother. After their parents' deaths, the brothers were the only family each had left. Regardless of their differences, Luisa had thought that William, or rather Brother William, as a man of religion, would feel a sense of duty in attending his only brother's wedding. It surprised her that he didn't. George couched his disappointment in anger and indifference.

———◆———

"So, Lou, how's it going?"

Luisa reclined deeper into the chair of the fashionably smart café on Rue de Namur. She stared at her girlfriend over a coffee cup. "Okay, I guess. For brothers who haven't seen each other in five years."

"I know you were worried. Frankly, I was a bit surprised to get your call. Thought you'd be busy with hosting duties."

"Walk did me good. I needed a break."

"That doesn't sound very promising."

Luisa put down her coffee and smoothed her hair. "I don't know, Kathrin. George and William…er, I mean Brother William," she added with a smile, "have a complicated relationship. They go from being chums reminiscing about the past to sniping. I don't know whether to join in the fun or take cover from the crossfire."

"Has it always been like this?"

Luisa shrugged. "From what George says, yes. But even he's adult enough to say there are two sides to every story. If they weren't brothers, I doubt they'd be friends."

"Any idea what's causing the row? Family squabbles usually run deepest of all."

Luisa cradled her chin. "Well, I'm rather new to the Hood family. But I'd say there's a degree of sibling rivalry, jealousy…"

"Sounds like any family," Kathrin said, slipping a forkful of carrot muffin into her mouth.

"This goes deeper. The worst lurks under the surface—George's views of organized religion, William's animosity toward his brother's work, the ex-wife. Half the time I feel everything's going great, only to learn later from George that he and his brother were engaged in submarine warfare. It's exhausting."

"I'm sorry. Our spare bedroom's at your disposal," Kathrin added with a laugh.

Luisa heaved a sigh. "Hope it doesn't come to that."

Kathrin leaned forward, a look of concern on her face. "Oh no, Lou. Is it really that serious?"

"It feels as if William brought Kay with him on holiday. In one volley, he suggested that George married her only to spite him. But the worst part of all is that George has started taking his frustrations with his brother out on me. Now, he's too busy to visit my family in Antwerp next month. Said I can go alone." Nibbling her fingernail, Luisa's gaze wandered out the window.

Since William's arrival four days prior, Luisa had done her best to make him feel welcome despite his loyalties toward George's ex-wife. If he considered Luisa *the other woman,* he didn't let on. Rather, he used Kay's name as a tactical weapon in skirmishes with his brother. He took great pleasure in boasting about her life since the divorce— "Kay's never been happier, prettier, or more successful and confident." William made her out to be a goddess, saint, and woman of the year. In spite of his irksome references to Kay, Luisa hated lying to her brother-in-law about how and when she and George had met.

William was clearly jealous of his younger brother's material success. He spoke sarcastically about George and Luisa's jet-set lifestyle while bemoaning his own meager finances. She had noticed the way he studied their apartment when he first arrived. It was less what he said and more what he didn't. Everyone who entered their flat was struck by the panoramic views of the ponds, not to mention the stunning architectural features of the flat and Luisa's tasteful decorations. Instead, William pointed out troubles with the plumbing, the small closets, and flaws with the floor plan. His bed and guest room were *adequate.* He showed little interest in their personal lives, calling their busy social calendar and extensive travels *nice* but no doubt *tiresome* after a while.

Luisa's allegiance was with her husband, of course. But George wasn't guiltless. He took great pleasure pointing out to his brother the many recent scandals dogging the Catholic Church. He had never understood William's embrace of organized religion. Hovering somewhere between atheist and agnostic, George felt that William squandered his life. In that regard, the brothers' parents were very much aligned. Their parents, George told her, pushed both sons to make something of their lives. Whereas they showered George with praise for his career in business, they perceived William's pursuit of a religious vocation as foolish, even self-indulgent—"a terrible waste."

George resented William for abandoning their parents when they most needed their sons, at the end when their mother was wracked with cancer and their father debilitated by Alzheimer's. "That's not the behavior of a so-called Christian," George often said to her. Luisa hoped they could survive William's visit without George repeating that complaint to his brother. George also felt that William failed him as an older brother. Instead of paving the way forward, William's path led toward the "dead end of religion."

"Where are they—now, I mean?" Kathrin's voice rose over the din as the café began to fill with the bustling lunch crowd of office workers, tourists, and shoppers.

"Sent them off to Brugge. I bowed out. Let them bond or bicker by themselves. Said I needed to run some errands before our road trip."

"Road trip?"

"I booked a Trappistes and Trenches tour for the three of us. It's only two days and nights. We pick it up in Ieper. Gives us all a chance to get out of the house, show Brother William some of the Flemish countryside. Thought he might appreciate the history and Trappist tours. The beer angle was the only way to lure George near a monastery."

Luisa approached the hotel breakfast table, scrutinizing the faces of her husband and brother-in-law over a vase of fresh flowers. It was her method of forecasting the volatile familial climate. Smiles, cordial banter, and the occasional laugh informed her of temperate conditions—at least for the moment. "You should see the square," she said, taking a seat at the table. "Full of vintage automobiles. Bentleys, I think. George just loves old cars." She turned toward William. "Do you as well?"

His face turned dour. "You in the market for a Bentley, George?"

Luisa preempted her husband. "Oh, no, George wants the new Mercedes. Two-door coupe with super—" The blush rising in George's cheeks informed her of her faux pas.

How could I be so stupid? She turned toward William, feigning an innocent smile. "Of course, they're all just silly automobiles. So how's the breakfast?"

George dabbed his mouth with a napkin. "Delicious. You really picked a first-class hotel, honey."

William cleared his throat, drawing Luisa's expectant gaze. "I really wish you'd let me pay for my room and this tour."

George glared at his brother. "That's not what Luisa asked, William."

Luisa made a tight-lipped smile, hoping to conceal her cringing embarrassment.

William stiffened. "Please excuse me, dear brother. Breakfast is fabulous, magnificent. Dear Luisa, I've never had better scrambled eggs in my life. First class all the way. Thank you both for your generosity."

Luisa sensed her husband bristle. She didn't want the tour to start off on such bad footing. The car ride from Brussels to Ieper had been bad enough with an argument about their parents' estate. George had told her that William resented his being named executor. William felt that the privilege belonged to him as the older brother.

Luisa affected a chipper tone as she pulled papers from her purse. "Look what I have: maps of our tour. They've done a good job of balancing history and refreshment. Just when we get tired of war, we stop for vespers and beer. And tonight we're back in Ieper for Last Post. I've always wanted to see that."

George snapped at her. "Why do you insist on calling it Ieper?"

Hurt and angered, she glared at her husband. "Because that's the town's name."

"Americans, most people, really, know it as Ypres," George said, accentuating and flubbing the French pronunciation.

"Well, it's a Flemish town, not a French one. And most Americans can't even call it Ypres," she said parroting his bad French accent. "Best your countrymen could do was call it Wipers."

William let out a bellow of a laugh. "She's got you there, Georgie."

Pulling her pink sweater tightly around her, Luisa watched as George and his brother wandered separately among the white rectangular gravestones. After they left the hotel and boarded the tour bus, a dense cloud cover moved in quickly, bringing with it a chilling wind and a hint of precipitation. Although ill-prepared for the climatic change, Luisa considered the dreary atmosphere fitting for the first stop of their tour.

Essex Farm Cemetery was two miles outside town. The area around Ieper had seen some of the First World War's fiercest battles. The cemetery, located on the site of a Canadian field hospital, contained the remains of more than one thousand fallen Commonwealth soldiers. On the exact spot in 1915, after the death of his friend and countryman in the Second Battle of Ieper, Canadian military doctor and artillery commander Lieutenant-Colonel John McCrae penned the poem, "In Flanders Fields."

Staring at the marble monument's brass plaque, Luisa recited the poem's first lines, "*In Flanders fields the poppies blow, / Between the crosses, row on row….*"

"Somber, isn't it?"

Luisa turned to find her brother-in-law. She handed him a tissue to dab his moist eyes. "My poor little country. Too many wars," Luisa said. "Why can't they all just leave us alone?" She held back her own sniffles. "What a terrible waste." The words echoed in her head. They sounded trite, inadequate. Everyone—wise men and fools—always talked about the awful waste and destruction of war. But that universal lament never stopped the killing.

William put his arm around her shoulders. "The pope says that many people don't want peace because they earn their livings making weaponry. In that case, dear Luisa, war will always be with us because of profiteers like—"

"Like *me*. Is that what you were going to say?"

Both turned to George. Luisa found her husband's expression harsh, a hint of red rising in his cheeks. Luisa recognized something more. Redness around his eyes betrayed the fact that the cemetery had also brought him to tears. But he was too proud to show his vulnerability, especially in front of his brother. Her husband, she knew, struggled with the moral conflicts of his job, guarding his feelings from all except her.

William released Luisa. "That's not what I was going to say. But if your guilty conscience wants to put words into my mouth, so be it. You've always acted as if you were the older brother."

"Well, if you hadn't abandoned Mom and Dad to pursue—"

Luisa threw her arms around her husband and kissed his cheek. "Please, dear. Not here," she added, scanning the gravestones.

She didn't have to say anymore. Both brothers, she felt, understood the unseemliness of bringing petty family arguments to hallowed ground. Pulling the brothers to her sides, she interlocked arms. The trio walked in silence back to the small tour bus.

Luisa and the brothers stood with the rest of their group on a gravel footpath on the grounds of the handsome Saint Sixtus Abbey. The vibrant green of the courtyard's lawn harmonized with the white brick of the three-story abbey. The building, adorned with cathedral windows and charcoal-gray shingles, had a simple beauty, a serenity that complemented its purpose.

The guide explained the history of the abbey, home to two dozen Trappist monks as well as the Westvleteren Brewery. The monks, originally from the Flemish region of France, founded the abbey in 1831 and began brewing beer seven years later. They offered three brews with varying alcohol content.

"The only brewery where Trappist monks still brew," the guide added. "Westvleteren 12 is the most potent. With strict production limits, it's also the most highly prized. As a matter of fact, they limit purchases to two cases. Customers order via the brewery's *beerphone*. One order every sixty days per license plate and telephone number. Thinking of cheating?" he added with a dramatic scowl. "Don't mess with monks." The group of Americans, Australians, and Irish laughed.

The guide gestured toward the brewery's modern annex, which housed an upscale restaurant and gift shop. "Now let's have lunch. Try a beer, or all three. Afterward we can go to the chapel for prayers. The chants aren't to be missed. But remember, those caught nodding off are at the mercy of the monks."

Inside the crowded dining room, the smell of roasted meats and vegetables mingled with the unmistakable fragrance of hops. Luisa, William, and George found themselves at the end of the long wooden table at which the tour group had gathered. Luisa was pleased with the brothers' playful mood as they recalled a crazy aunt who drank beer for breakfast.

Luisa lifted her glass, its shape a chalice, the brewery's signature design. "To family."

The brothers, smiling and cheerful, lifted their glasses, repeating her toast.

William puckered his lips. "Wow! This really is potent."

George laughed. "Nearly eleven percent alcohol. The fine monks know what they're doing."

Luisa snickered, lifting her chalice filled with blond beer. "This is what the monks drink. Closer to six percent."

"So they claim, so they claim," George replied with a grin. "And Aunty Janet's beer binges were purely medicinal. Gotta hand it to these fellas. Flee the pressures of modern society and brew beer. Drink as much as they can and sell the rest. Bet they have comfy recliners and satellite TV too. I know plenty of guys who'd kill for this cushy life."

Aware of the lobbed incendiary, Luisa uttered a polite laugh. "I'm anxious to hear the chants," she said, trying to draw William into the conversation. His expression remained frozen in a tight-lipped smile. She recognized that ploy as one used by her husband: a slow simmer, an internal struggle between outburst and discretion.

George hoisted his nearly empty chalice. "Count me out. This is the closest I come to church. What a racket—like all organized religion." Luisa caught his last words even though they were delivered under his breath. She just hoped William was too busy answering a question from the Irish woman at his side to have heard.

"What was that, dear brother?"

Luisa's stomach sank. She hoped her husband was tactful enough not to repeat himself. She was wrong. The beer emboldened him.

"Face it. Organized religion is a sham. Take this place. Profiting off of alcohol."

"I don't think they actually profit," Luisa said, trying to play peacekeeper.

George scoffed. "Really? Look around. State-of-the-art. Our guide says the good monks increase production for renovations. Sell their beer online in America. Hell," George added with a boisterous laugh, "tell me how that's any different from Amazon and OPEC?"

"Honey, please."

William held up his palm. "That's all right, Luisa. I know this is directed at me. For what I said back at the cemet—"

George leaned across the table, his gaze focused on his brother. "You want to talk about warmongering. How many wars have been fought in the name of religion? Think about that before you go all holier-than-thou on me."

William smirked. "Kay's always said you have the most miserable temper."

George stiffened at the mention of his ex-wife. "Share this with dear Kay: Luisa and I didn't meet *after* I moved to Brussels. She was a flight attendant on my Washington to Brussels run…*every week*. Layovers were pretty damn good too."

Luisa wanted to scream. How dare George use her like that, a weapon to lash out at his brother, especially after he had insisted she lie repeatedly about how they'd met? Instead of screaming, she started to cry. "I'm sorry."

"What are you sorry for?" Her husband's tone was harsh.

"Oh, George. Sometimes you can be so cruel."

William shook his head. "Yes, George, so very, very cruel."

Luisa turned to her brother-in-law. "You too, *Brother* William. You're not without blame. You two behave like spoiled brats. Don't care who you hurt." Luisa walked away, muttering under her breath, "I'm sick of you both."

Luisa decided she was going to Last Post with or without George and William. Since returning to the hotel, the brothers had sulked like pouting toddlers. William said he wasn't hungry yet Luisa heard room service delivering a tray to his room. She was still processing what he had told her in confidence while the two waited in the monastery's chapel for prayers. She believed he was contrite for his bad behavior and felt sorry for her after George's cruel outburst over lunch. Perhaps the chapel stoked his conscience. Still, William's confession shocked her. He faced the biggest conflict of his life. He was considering leaving the church to marry Kay.

At dinner, George barely spoke. When he did, she wished he hadn't. His tone was surly, confrontational. He was looking for a fight. She recognized the mix of anger and embarrassment in his reaction when she demanded an apology for the way he'd been treating her since William's arrival. When she asked him to accompany her to Last Post, he replied that he preferred to watch television.

Clothed against the cold and drizzle, Luisa stepped outside the hotel. She paused to take in the town's magnificent belfry and cloth hall. Reconstruction efforts had restored the medieval structures, proud symbols of the town's history, to their prewar majesty. She wondered whether the brothers would be on speaking terms when they visited the building's First World War museum the next day. *If not, I'll go alone. I'm through playing peacekeeper.*

As she made her way across the wide square, lights from bustling cafés sparkled on the damp cobblestones. *Ieper is a pretty little town.* She could hardly imagine that German shelling had reduced the town to rubble only a century before. Churchill, she learned in school, proposed that Ieper should forever remain in ruins, a monument to the sacrifice of British forces. By that logic, she thought, most of Belgium would lie in ruins, shrine to legions of foreign armies that ravaged her country in pursuit of greater glories. Inhabitants of Ieper, however, were determined to reclaim their lives and town. Ieper was a microcosm for all of Belgium, a nation that persevered through adversity. Luisa swelled with pride for her heritage.

She reached the edge of the square. Spotlights lit up the brilliant white facade of the Menin Gate, a monument to fallen soldiers whose remains were never identified. More than fifty-four thousand names were etched into the marble. Police cordoned off the road and spectators gathered under the memorial's barrel-vaulted ceiling as they'd done every night for decades.

Luisa peered over her shoulder. She hoped to see George and William. But they weren't there. Neither, she concluded, could set aside their brooding rivalry. Sharing their inner conflicts could have facilitated reconciliation. Pride and secrecy kept the brothers apart.

She turned to face the buglers. Members of the local fire brigade played the final haunting bars of "Last Post." In battle, the bugle call had announced the security of camp for the night and summoned absent comrades. Whether wounded on the battlefield or simply lost, soldiers followed the call to find safety and rest for the night.

The bugles fell silent; the crowd remained hushed—no applause, no cheers.

As Luisa strolled back among the crowd, tears streaked her cheeks. She recalled the last lines of McCrae's poem. *We shall not sleep, though poppies grow / In Flanders fields.*

She looked across the dark square to the lights of her hotel. "A terrible waste, indeed."

Lockdown

"Good God, dear brother, are you insane?"

At the sound of the familiar voice speaking in Arabic, Hasan looked up from his iPad. His older brother Kadar stood over him, a scowl on his face. "What possessed you to come here?" the older man added.

As his brother spoke, Hasan noted another emotion blending into his expression but couldn't decipher it. Hasan shrugged. "I come to this café every Monday. You know that."

Kadar's appearance, more formal than usual, surprised Hasan. The shirt and tie from an Italian designer were his brother's favorites. The suit, gray silk hand-tailored by their favorite uncle back in Beirut, was his best. In Hasan's closet hung an identical garment, which he wore for the occasional job interview or, more often, to impress the ladies.

Kadar pulled out a chair from the small table and sat across from Hasan. After scanning the crowded café, he spoke in a hushed tone. "You think it wise…especially today?"

"Why whisper?" Hasan asked with a smirk. "I doubt these people understand Arabic. And if you're referring to Paris—"

Kadar leaned over the table, his face reddening. "Yes, I'm talking about Paris. And now, Brussels."

Two days before, on Saturday morning, the brothers had awoken, like many others across Europe, to news that Belgian authorities raised the security threat level to the highest possible for the Brussels region. Officials declared as *serious and imminent* the risk of a terrorist attack like the one that had struck Paris only a week before. The well-coordinated siege of the French capital on that crisp November night raised the specter of an escalation in terrorist activity. Shockwaves reverberated across the globe. Ten days later, the death toll in Paris stood at one hundred and thirty. With hundreds more seriously injured, news outlets predicted the casualty count would rise.

"Paris has nothing to do with me…with *us*. Neither does any of this." Hasan nodded toward the café's large front window. Chaussée de Charleroi, one of Brussels' main thoroughfares, was nearly deserted. Replacing shoppers and office workers, soldiers wearing camouflage uniforms and carrying automatic weapons patrolled the pavements. Instead of trams, tanks and armored vehicles rattled along the streets. The scene was eerie, surreal. Anxiety hung in the air like fog. The city descended into a state of suspended animation, a centuries-old European capital on lockdown.

Kadar tensed. The vein in his forehead became more pronounced. His dark eyes lasered on his younger brother. "Don't be stupid. This *always* has to do with us. Whether you wish to see it, we're guilty by association."

Though Hasan shook his head in disagreement with his brother's passionate assertion, he wasn't naïve. Prejudice and bigotry were real. Outside the Middle East, people regarded "their kind" with suspicion, scorning and even vilifying their customs and religion. Suspicion and distrust had become more pronounced after deadly terrorist attacks struck New York, Madrid, and London during the early years of the century. Two attacks in Paris in the last ten months further stoked anxieties among the populace. The growing menace of the Islamic State and reports of European sympathizers flocking to join the radical cause didn't help matters. In recent months, record inflows of migrants and refugees from the Middle East and Africa brought more unwanted attention to their people. Local television streamed daily videos of the swelling refugee encampment that sprang up near the

Brussels-North railway station. Political parties on the right ascended throughout Europe on populist platforms with fearful rhetoric about Trojan horses and shouts of "Enough is enough!"

For Hasan, somehow, Belgium felt different. He sensed a passive acceptance of Muslims in his adopted land. The laissez-faire attitude seemed cultural, perhaps even a by-product of the nation's loose federation of proud and fiercely independent German, French, and Flemish speakers. He found Belgians inward-looking, fractured along language and ethnic lines—more clanlike or tribal than he expected. A foreigner was no more suspicious or unwanted than a native countryman with a different mother tongue. What did it really mean to be Belgian anymore? One didn't wander far in Brussels without encountering people of every race and nationality.

Despite his optimism, Hasan remained cautious. Tolerance within his host country continued in spite of recent incidents within its borders. These included a fatal attack on Brussels' Jewish museum and the discovery of a terrorist sleeper cell operating out of the eastern city of Verviers. And thanks to the media and right-wing alarmists, the world knew that Belgium sent more jihadists to fight for ISIS on a per-capita basis than any other European country. How long, therefore, Hasan wondered, would the welcome mat remain out? Hate and fear were a toxic mix.

At Sumatra, the modern café where Kadar found him, Hasan always felt at home. The café's energetic owner, Adelia, herself a Muslim émigrée from a central Asian republic, had a gracious welcome for all. Westernized in speech and dress, Adelia had married an Iowa farm boy. Her café was clean and efficient, more American than European. She imported her bagels and marketing tactics from New York. One wall featured a massive photograph of the Brooklyn Bridge while the background music featured a heavy mix of American pop standards.

Like Hasan, Adelia embraced her adopted culture. Coffee and a new baby were her primary passions. Tolerance seemed as natural to her as customer service and warm hospitality in the Muslim tradition.

In addition to being a kind person and a savvy entrepreneur, Adelia was a role model. Hasan also hoped to immerse himself in Western culture, Brussels just a first step to something bigger, a life, perhaps, in Canada or the United States. His brother Kadar shared that dream, or so Hasan thought.

As the brothers continued to chat, Hasan understood his brother's out-of-place formality. The emotions firing within Kadar were unmistakable, revealing themselves in his face and tone. "So, is that why you're all dressed up?"

Kadar bristled. "What?"

Hasan tugged his brother's lapel. "Concealing your shame behind fine silk."

Batting away Hasan's hand, Kadar's expression hardened. "I'm not ashamed."

"No? Then why be shocked to find me here? Should we cower behind closed doors till this threat blows over?" It was Hasan's turn to glare across the table. "Got news for you, dear brother: there will be more threats, attacks, and killings."

"More reason to use common sense." Pulling cigarettes from his pocket, Kadar's fingers fidgeted with the pack. "What does any of that have to do with my suit?"

"Tell me, Kadar, tell me you didn't put on your fine clothes to throw off suspicion? You pretending to be a bigwig banker, some Middle East oil executive?" Hasan's finger poked the air over the table. "You're not comfortable in your own skin."

Hasan braced for an enraged response, but a blush in his brother's cheek told him he'd hit his mark. He loved his older brother but knew that shame and guilt shackled him. A short temper betrayed a conflict that raged within. It wasn't simply their Muslim heritage. No, Kadar also bore guilt as an eldest son sponging off his parents. Their mother and father had funded their adult sons' move to Brussels two years earlier. Survivors of the bitter civil war that gripped Lebanon for fifteen years, they wanted a better life for their sons. Despite infirmities, the parents wired from Beirut a monthly allowance that covered their sons' living expenses. These included rent for a small flat in a squalid part of Brussels, home to the brothers as well as Kadar's wife and their infant daughter. Both brothers, but especially Kadar, craved their father's approval. That, they believed, would only come when they proved themselves successful businessmen.

Hasan's suspicions ran even deeper. He sensed that Kadar harbored a secret, something so dark and dangerous that he didn't dare broach the topic with his brother.

"Your coffee." The young server with braided hair and thick eyeliner spoke in English as she slid a cappuccino in front of Hasan. A heart-shaped design decorated the coffee's creamy top.

Hasan grinned. The young women who worked in the café often flirted with him. He wasn't vain; he simply understood that females found him attractive. He had a lean physique and worked out regularly. His eyes, a shade or two lighter brown than his brother's, contrasted with his classic Middle Eastern features including thick black hair styled after a celebrity footballer. Hasan shared his brother's taste for designer fashions such as the snug trousers and slim-fit shirt from a top English designer he wore that day under a black leather jacket. Women often called him "Handsome" to his face and whispered to each other in voices loud enough for him to hear that he was a hunk or a hottie.

Hasan lifted the cup and winked at the server in acknowledgment of her handiwork.

"Let me know if you want anything else," she said before turning to Kadar. "Nice suit. The usual?" she asked, brushing against his thigh.

Kadar stiffened; his smile looked forced. "Y…yes, p…please."

Hasan nodded toward the retreating server. "You see? Yvette couldn't care less if we're Lebanese or Latvian. She just—"

"Wants to get into *your* pants," Kadar said, with a scowl. "And by that proud grin on your face, I'm guessing she already has. No need to lie. I see it in your eyes."

Feeling his cheeks warm, Hasan wondered why. Sure he'd played around with Yvette as he'd done with many others since arriving in Brussels. He was young and not married, *yet*. His bachelor days were numbered though. His parents had arranged Kadar's marriage and were finalizing the selection of a bride for Hasan from a "suitable" family. Hasan hoped for a happy match, unlike his brother's experience. Hasan often came to Café Sumatra, as a matter of fact, to escape the crying baby and the bickering between Kadar and his wife, which had grown in frequency and intensity. Arguments concerning money and childcare had expanded into a broader range of topics, some too intimate for Hasan's liking including the couple's sexual relations. The glares that Kadar's wife shot her husband had turned from tired frustration to ice cold anger.

A sneer formed on Kadar's face. "Sure, maybe I wore my good suit to…to blend in. Show them we're not all animals. Less likely to be stopped by a storm trooper," Kadar added, gesturing out the window to a passing group of soldiers. "At least I'm not screwing every woman in Brussels who shows the least bit of interest. That's a reckless path toward acceptance. Not very honorable either."

Hasan was neither proud nor ashamed of his active libido. It just was. After all, wasn't that a Western virtue? That's what the movies portrayed anyway. Hasan shrugged off Kadar's barb, choosing discretion over a caustic rebuttal. He didn't want to destroy their relationship. Irreparable harm, he believed, was a single accusation away. Once uttered, the scorching words would scar like a red-hot branding iron.

Instead, Hasan squeezed his brother's arm and assumed a lighthearted tone. "Don't kid yourself, they'd want in your pants too if you weren't…already married. Especially in that suit. Women like a little danger. Why shouldn't I seize the opportunity? We're exotic, you and me. You see it in their eyes."

Kadar stood. The pack of cigarettes in his hand crackled in his grip. "You don't want to know what I see in their eyes." He turned, walking toward the café's back door and smoking terrace.

Waiting for his brother to return, Hasan scanned the café's other customers. With many businesses and the Metro closed due to the security threat, among the regular patrons were several unfamiliar faces. Newcomers pecked away at computers and conferenced on smart phones. Seated on the leather sofa was an American man Hasan recognized, the husband of a woman transferred to Brussels by a global accounting firm. With no work permit, the man spent his days chatting up staff and strangers in the café. He told Hasan that he spent most afternoons taking photos while the couple's children were in school. Today, he was conversing loudly with another café regular, a sarcastic Bulgarian who wrote screenplays in English. Like so many, they were talking about the security situation.

"Thinking of moving the family to Molenbeek," the Bulgarian said, referring to the Brussels commune where security forces traced clusters of terrorists and where the brothers also lived. "Probably the safest place in the city. A dog doesn't shit in its own crate."

The American chuckled. "Sally and I keep getting notes from folks back home wondering if we're okay. I laugh at them. Hey, don't get me wrong. We appreciate the concern. But they're living in Chicago, for Christ's sake. I can't check the Internet without reading about another dozen shootings in the Windy City."

Hasan wanted to jump into their conversation with *And they think Muslims are crude and violent*. Instead, he kept the thought to himself, simply smiling at his acquaintances. Kadar, he knew, wouldn't have been so discreet.

Around another table sat a group of flight attendants, male and female. Blue uniforms with maroon piping and striped jacket sleeves gave them away. Several weeks earlier, crew from the same American airline had struck up a conversation with Hasan in the café. He laughed to himself recalling the rivalry for his attention between a pretty blonde flight attendant from Mississippi and an impeccably groomed young man with a Boston accent. Hasan was flattered by the flirtations, but it was no contest. He enjoyed learning a few quaint idioms of America's

Deep South while sampling the plush bed and whirlpool tub of the posh hotel across the road where the crews laid over.

Today's group, however, seemed more anxious than that prior bunch—somber faces and hushed whispers. He understood their serious mood, given the security concerns. Hasan lamented that at Threat Level 4, even the flirtations of the sassiest flight attendants were also on lockdown.

Kadar returned from the outside terrace shaking his head. Reeking of cigarette smoke, he slid his phone on the table with such force it knocked the cup and saucer.

"*Now* what's wrong? Your expression's more sour than before."

Kadar groaned. "Moha called. He'll be here any minute."

"And?"

The appearance of Adelia, the café's owner, interrupted Kadar's reply. Her round, pale face usually sported a smile, but not this day. "Hi, guys." Her coal-black eyes and tone lacked their customary sparkle. "Good to see my regular customers. How go things?"

Kadar merely shrugged, leaving Hasan to speak. "Glad you're open. Most of the city's a ghost town."

Adelia sighed. "Costs don't shut down. Need to stay open…if I can." Lowering her voice, she relayed a story. Over the weekend, a stranger had come into the café and warned her staff that someone planned to shoot up the place. "'Just like Paris,' he said. He looked reasonably normal, but he sure scared the girls. Darya quit on the spot." Police deemed the threat as not credible. "But who knows? It's a crazy world," Adelia added, tilting her head back toward the counter. "That's why *he's* here."

After following Adelia's glance, the brothers eyed each other, concern on their faces. With the café packed, they hadn't noticed the blue-uniformed policeman before. Moha's imminent arrival wouldn't have caused worry under normal circumstances, but these weren't ordinary times.

With her hands on their shoulders, Adelia told the brothers she'd send over refills on the house.

"You see the cop?"

Hasan and Kadar looked up from their conversation. Moha's chubby, pockmarked face was gray, his lips quivering. His clothes always reeked of onions and tobacco.

The brothers were in business with Moha, a man several years older. The second-generation immigrant viewed laws as mere guidelines. Together, the three men traded in secondhand items from Brussels' robust expat community, a revolving door courtesy of NATO and the institutions of the European Union. The trio scoured moving sales and Internet auction sites for merchandise. Refurbished and repackaged items, including electronics and appliances, fetched a tidy profit. They dealt in cash, a bonus in tax-greedy Belgium although it meant dodging the eager Belgian tax man.

Their semi-legitimate business had another, illegal and highly lucrative, side. Using bribes and a network of associates to bypass customs laws, the partners had a robust export trade. Most items went to Lebanon. The biggest profits, however, came from trafficking to Gaza, running goods through the Israeli blockade.

Hasan argued with Kadar about the growth in illegal activity. Hasan understood his brother's need for additional income, and even enjoyed the financial rewards himself, but he feared that discovery would destroy any hope of migrating to America. Kadar's reply was always the same. "If they're going to judge us terrorists anyway, why not profit from their prejudice?"

Kadar kicked out an empty chair from the table. "Sit."

Moha took off his blue cargo jacket. Hasan noticed large perspiration rings under the arms of his shirt. "Relax," Hasan said. He nodded toward the stout, stern-faced policeman. "He's not here for us." He shared Adelia's story of the threat made to her staff, but beads formed on Moha's creased forehead anyway.

Kadar turned to Moha, whispering in Arabic. "Go ahead, tell him what you told me on the phone."

Moha took a napkin off the table to dab his beaded brow. "I had two women today, sellers with good merchandise. Wouldn't let me in. Guessing they saw me through the window. That's never happened before."

Hasan swatted the air above the table. "Is that all?"

"No, that's not all," Moha said, his eyes darting to and from the policeman. "My van is drawing soldiers' stares. Since all this threat level shit hit the fan, I've had over half a dozen cancellations. 'Too busy,' some say. 'Decided to sell elsewhere,' claim others. I know lies when I hear them."

Kadar pounded the table. "First they take our self-respect and now our livelihood. How do we survive if they won't do business with us? They think we're terrorists—every last one of us."

Hasan felt Kadar's harsh tone directed at him. "Calm down, brother," he said, glancing toward the policeman and back again. "This'll blow over. People are panicking, that's all. Wait for this lockdown to end. Money trumps bigotry and fear—*always*."

Kadar glared at his brother. "What if it doesn't? What if our goods supply dries up? We're screwed."

"We'll figure something out," Hasan said, though he hadn't a scrap of a plan. Secretly, he shared his brother's concern. They hoped to *end* reliance upon their parents' allowance, not ask for more. He recalled his sister-in-law's shrill voice carping at Kadar, "An honorable man and father provides for his family." Hasan saw, however, a silver lining—a possible ramping down of their illegal activities. Perhaps the brothers could open up a coffee shop of their own.

After downing an espresso, Moha rose from the table. Although he blamed his abrupt departure on a need to check on his van, Hasan knew better. He exchanged a knowing glance with his brother as a jittery Moha eyed the counter and muttered a profanity directed at the policeman.

Kadar came back from ordering another cup of coffee, shaking. His face was white; his eyes flashed with fury and fear. "Bloody faggot."

Hasan gasped. "Lower your voice." He waited for his brother to sit before whispering across the table in Arabic, "What the hell are you talking about?"

Kadar seethed. He motioned over his shoulder at the group of flight attendants. A few of them, Hasan noticed, stole furtive glances at the brothers. *This isn't good, not with that policeman.* Hasan repeated in an even lower voice, "What happened?"

Kadar's hands formed fists. He spoke through gritted teeth. "They look at you like you're an animal. Treat you like it too. Yet they're the filthy swine." Every muscle in his face tensed.

Hasan grabbed his brother's arm. "Come on. Let's go outside, grab a smoke."

On the terrace, the cool air acted as a calming agent. Hasan rubbed his brother's back, encouraging him to take deep breaths. Pulling out his cigarettes, Hasan took one and offered another to his brother. Kadar followed Hasan's lead, sitting beside him on the steps of the metal staircase that led down to the garden already shuttered for winter.

After a few silent minutes, Hasan spoke. "Tell me what happened."

Kadar shook his head. "I don't want to talk about it."

"Has something to do with the flight crew, doesn't it?"

Kadar remained silent. He exhaled the smoke from his cigarette and took another drag.

"Not budging till you tell me." Hasan's tone was a mix of firmness and compassion.

After rubbing his forehead, Kadar's hand came to rest covering his eyes.

Hasan squeezed his brother's shoulder. That simple gesture transported him back to childhood. The roles were reversed. Kadar, barely a teenager, comforted ten-year-old Hasan after a run-in with the neighborhood bully. At the time, Hasan was a slight boy, before the growth spurt and bodybuilding kick that made him bigger and stronger than Kadar. The bully, a young Hasan confessed through tears, had called him a homo, got the other boys to join in the taunting as well. Soon after that talk on the steps of their parents' store, Kadar beat the bully senseless. Hasan had never known his older brother—a bookish, sensitive boy—to fight prior to that incident. But afterward, Kadar changed. No longer sensitive or bookish, he went out of his way to prove his masculinity. He became a bully, provoking fights with weaker, effeminate boys.

Hasan squeezed his brother's shoulder harder. "Tell me what upset you."

Kadar took a deep breath. "One of the trolley dollies…hit on me."

"You sure?"

Kadar's reply came in the form of a cold glare.

"It's harmless, even flattering. He meant no harm."

"It's disgusting." Kadar shook. Hasan didn't know if he was trembling with anger or fighting back tears. "I should beat him to a pulp."

"Listen. It's not disgusting, sick, dirty…any of that. You forget the video?" As part of the immigration process, applicants watched an official Belgian film that highlighted the nation's collective values. Scenes of same-sex couples appeared among other samples of Belgian life.

Kadar turned away, forcing Hasan's hand from his shoulder. "A video doesn't make it right."

Hasan chose his words carefully. "Dearest brother. I love our new home as much as I love you."

"What the hell does that mean?"

"We clamor for acceptance and tolerance. But we must be willing to accept and tolerate…others as well as ourselves."

"I can't."

"But I can and do. So should you. I wish nothing more for you than happiness, for you to be comfortable in your own skin."

"So you said."

"I'm not talking about your suit." Brussels, Hasan knew, wasn't alone in lockdown. His brother hid his sexuality behind fortifications. And like the city, Kadar would need time and assurances of safety to shed layers of self-imposed security. Kadar's emergence from his secret bunker would be deliberate, slow. "Dear brother," Hasan said, "please accept yourself for who and what you are."

Kadar snuffed out his cigarette. His face tensed; his hands formed fists. Surging with emotion, he stifled his tears. Hasan embraced his quaking brother. He wouldn't reject Kadar any more than he could abandon Brussels and his dreams of a better life. Family transcended borders, culture, even religion. Hasan would remain at his brother's side, helping him move beyond the shame and fears that kept his spirit in lockdown.

Stuff of Dreams

The Legend of Beatrijs and the Virgin Mary

Brussels' Church of Our Blessed Lady of the Sablon is a Gothic masterpiece with an origin shrouded in mystery. According to the legend, in 1348, the Virgin Mary appeared to Beatrijs Soetkens, a devout young woman from Antwerp. With no explanation, the Virgin instructed her to steal a statue dedicated to Mary from a local church and transport it to Brussels. Once there the Virgin added, the Crossbow Guild would honor and protect the piece.

As directed, Beatrijs snatched the religious statue. She journeyed to Brussels by boat—a miraculous feat, given the fact that no direct water link from Antwerp existed at that time. Beatrijs accomplished her mission with the aid and protection of a boatman and a group of crossbowmen. The magnificent church in the Grand Sablon that survives to this day stands on the site of an earlier fourteenth-century chapel of the Crossbow Guild, the exact spot where Beatrijs' incredible journey ended.

The Crossbow Guild venerated their patroness by making a procession called an Ommegang. Guild members paraded the statue of the Virgin Mary through the cobblestone streets of medieval Brussels. The Ommegang tradition continues to the present day in the form of a colorful civic pageant.

Contemporary visitors to the Church of Our Blessed Lady

encounter two statues. One is a replica of the statue brought by Beatrijs Soetkens. (Calvinist zealots destroyed the original in the sixteenth century.) The other statue depicts the legend. Prominently placed in a side aisle is a longboat displaying colorful likenesses of the Madonna and Child along with Beatrijs and the boatman.

Was Beatrijs' vision a veritable miracle or merely a young woman's fabrication to provide cover for escape and larceny? Perhaps Beatrijs' bold odyssey itself, rather than the statue, warrants attention and admiration. Maybe she was simply a courageous young woman whose daring mission was a journey of self-discovery and personal growth. Individual interpretation keeps the legend alive and interesting to this very day.

Beatrice and Her Miraculous Journey

"No, no!" Beatrice Sterk wailed. The young woman was somewhere in the netherworld between sleep and consciousness. Time was as fluid as a surrealist clock. When she kicked the blanket and rolled onto her side, her charm bracelet clanked on the metal bed frame, plunging her into yet another dream.

Beatrice found herself at the wedding of a childhood friend, an actual event that had occurred earlier that spring. As often happens in dreams, the setting was illogical, absurd. Instead of the fancy restaurant where the real reception took place, revelers mingled on a three-tiered wedding cake, a replica of the very cake that Beatrice had created for her friend's wedding. On the bottom layer, Beatrice sat pouting in a rose of pink frosting. She gazed up to the pedestal on the top tier. Joost was handsome in a black tuxedo. His dark hair was slicked back, and a diamond stud glistened on his earlobe.

Beatrice, now in her mid-twenties, had known Joost since they were children growing up together in a small Flemish village. In third grade, when he pushed her on a playground swing, she granted him her first kiss. By the time the friends entered high school, she'd given him her virginity. In her diary she wrote that she loved Joost more than music, poetry, drawing, even life itself. She yearned to become, Mrs. Joost Peeters. After high school, the pair drifted apart. Joost went away to university and Beatrice put her dreams on hold to assume the place of her ill mother in the family bakery.

Atop the cake in Beatrice's dream, Joost stood next to his bride Liv, a stunning fair-haired Scandinavian doctor. She worked at a clinic catering to troubled youth, the very place where the couple had met. An aspiring lawyer, Joost took pro-bono cases for his firm. Often, he needed to consult the clinic's staff to mount defenses for clients, most of whom were merely a few years younger than he.

In the dream, as she had done at the actual wedding, Liv wore a traditional Norwegian wedding outfit. The most unique feature of her ensemble was the headdress, a silver crown worn in place of a veil. Small spoon-shaped bangles of gold ringed the seven-point filigree crown. Whenever the bride moved her head, the bangles chimed. Liv explained to her guests that the melodic sound warded off evil spirits. The more she danced at her reception, the happier and more secure the marriage would be.

The crown both fascinated and repulsed Beatrice. It was a reminder that a foreign interloper had snatched away her most cherished dream, Joost, the love of her life.

Without knowing how she got there, Beatrice herself was atop the cake, standing beside Joost. His blue eyes gazed at her lovingly—her dream come true. *Oh but yes*, she thought, *only the crown will ensure our happiness*. Beatrice reached forward to snatch the bangled crown from off the bride's head. Liv stumbled backward. Joost's kind smile vanished; shock swept across his face. He glared at Beatrice. "You're drunk!" he shouted, shoving her from his side. He grabbed Liv's hand mere seconds before she tumbled off the cake. Beatrice, teetering on her feet, stumbled toward the cake's edge.

Beatrice awoke in a fit, her feet shuffling to retain their footing on the imagined wedding cake. She tried to push the nightmare from her head. Her heart raced, her breathing labored. Squinting, she attempted to make sense of her situation.

Where the hell am I?

When Beatrice first arrived in Antwerp, she had the good fortune of crashing on the floor of a stranger's tiny studio. But six weeks later, the free-spirited tattoo artist kicked Beatrice out to make room for a new boyfriend from Belgrade. Beatrice didn't have enough money for alcohol, weed, the occasional coke fix, and a roof over her head. Most temporary housing agencies, including churches, demanded that she abandon her nasty habits while she waited for a permanent placement. Summer wasn't the worst time to take shelter on the streets, she figured. The narrow lanes and alleys of Antwerp's old city center provided an abundance of drug sources and drinking companions.

Beatrice spent two weeks on the streets when a fast-moving front swept in from the North Sea bringing a mix of rain and unseasonably cool temperatures for early July. Cold air was one thing, but driving rain was quite another. The unrelenting storm forced Beatrice to seek shelter. From past experience, she knew that hostels asked fewer questions than social agencies and churches. There were rules, but commercial interests trumped morality. As long as she was quiet and didn't cause any trouble, no one would bother her.

Beatrice headed to a seedy patch of the city near the red-light district and bustling waterfront. She hadn't taken money for sex, yet. But as Europe's second biggest cargo port, Antwerp promised a steady and eager clientele should she need to. Beatrice chewed half a dozen breath mints as she neared the address scribbled on her palm.

The petite Asian woman who ran the hostel had a perpetual smile that looked unnatural. Taking the fifteen euros in banknotes that Beatrice scraped together for a single room, the woman handed back three coins. "Save your money, girlie," she said with an exaggerated wink. "You sleep in dormitory. Only one other girl tonight and she in own world—*la la la la*...." The grinning woman cupped her ears with imaginary headphones and bobbled her head.

Beatrice didn't argue. Three euros would cover the hostel's hot breakfast option. Her stomach growled just thinking about it. She couldn't remember the last time she ate a warm breakfast. She could barely recall her last substantial meal. The proprietor exchanged words with a fellow in an Eastern language before the tight-lipped Asian man led Beatrice down the hallway. Downstairs dormitories were co-ed. Private rooms and gender-segregated dormitories occupied the upper floors. The ground floor reminded her of a high school corridor. Staff tried too hard to camouflage with lemon cleaning solutions the earthy aroma that mixed with scents of fast food, stale cigarettes, and body odor. A guy and a girl covered in tattoos congregated outside the communal toilet. They met her glance with blank expressions.

The Asian man stopped. He nodded toward a set of stairs. "Up one flight, first floor. Man dorm right, woman left. You have good sleep."

After a much-needed stop at the toilet, Beatrice pushed open the door to the women's dormitory. The beige, unadorned room had a dozen metal-framed beds, each with an orange blanket. The room's only other occupant, the girl mentioned by the hostel keeper, reclined on the bed closest to the door. Beatrice figured she was about twenty, no more than three or four years younger than she. Wearing ear buds, the girl's bare feet kept time to her private music, rattling the metal bed frame. Visible above one ankle was a tattoo of a pink rose. Her head, topped by a kinky-blonde nest of hair, didn't turn when Beatrice entered the room. A smart phone in her hand consumed her attention.

Beatrice walked to the corner of the room farthest from her roommate. Twisting to remove her red backpack, Beatrice dropped the heavy bag onto the bed. The rucksack, along with a bulging shoulder bag bought from a Nigerian street peddler, contained what was left of her possessions. Two months earlier, upon arriving at Antwerp's central railway station, she had made the mistake of leaving her suitcase unattended inside a coffee shop. She was gone only a matter of seconds, a dash to the toilet to pop a pill with a generous swig of vodka. But that was ample time for a thief to strike. The two policemen weren't sympathetic, raising eyebrows at her carelessness and exchanging glances when her words slurred on alcohol-laced breath. Her plight, however, drew the attention of a young tattooed stranger in the coffee shop. The woman invited Beatrice to crash on her apartment floor—until her new Serbian boyfriend entered the picture and pushed Beatrice to the streets.

Settling into her temporary refuge, Beatrice kicked off her shoes and nudged them beneath the hostel bed. As she sat on the firm mattress, a whiff of alcohol turned her attention to the other side of the room. She looked up just in time to see her roommate stash a bottle under the bedcovers. It wasn't wine but something stronger. The girl glared until Beatrice turned away. But hers hadn't been a judgmental sneer. That sniff was all Beatrice needed to jolt awake her own desire.

Beatrice thrust her hand into her backpack and pulled out a paper sack—inside, a half-empty bottle of cheap vodka. Disrobing down to her bra and panties, she slipped under the covers. She didn't want to think that the warm bed was only temporary. She didn't want to think about her failed past or bleak future. She didn't want to have to think about anything. Wriggling closer to the wall, she took a swig from the bottle. Tilting her head backward into the flat pillow, she sighed. The vodka would soon numb her pesky thoughts and silence the muffled voices of two men audible through paper-thin walls.

———※———

Beatrice's dream of Joost and the silver wedding crown was only one of many that night in the hostel. After two weeks sleeping on the streets, her new, safe, and comfortable surroundings were tinder for a mind flickering with agitation. Under the influence of alcohol, dreams and reality blended together like the confluence of two great rivers. Beatrice floated on a current of truth and fantasy, each at once distinct and indistinguishable. In this fluid state of consciousness, disembodied voices drifted in the air above her. Imagination and memory gave the voices human form.

"No, dude, it's either the stash or the cash. We can't be caught with both."

"You gotta be f—in' kiddin' me, man. You expect us to leave twenty thousand euros somewhere in Antwerp? That's f—in' nuts."

"Calm down, dude. Coke's worth six times that to Raphael."

"Still don't like leavin' that much cash here. I say we take the money and disappear."

"You don't mess with Raphael."

"Well, where we gonna hide this cash? Can't leave it here, man. Too many losers lookin' to score."

"I got a plan."

Beatrice knew where the dream was heading, and she didn't like it. She hated that part of dreaming. Knowing what was coming but being powerless to stop it. She gnashed her teeth; her body stiffened. This series started out differently, but all of her nightmares ended the same. At any second, she and her father would pop into this scene with the two stoned drug dealers. Her father would confront her about the stolen money. "Five thousand euros, Bea, five thousand euros. Your mother and I put our whole life into the bakery—for you. This is how you repay us—stealing for drugs and alcohol?" The nightmares always ended with her slow-motion escape pursued by her angry father, her sobbing late mother, and the police.

In the physical world of real life, Beatrice had run away to Antwerp. If only her tortured conscience could have escaped as well.

Beatrice waited, but she didn't appear in the dream. Nor did her father. Still, the voices of the two druggies continued.

"So here's what we're going to do, dude. We hide the money in the cathedral."

"Cathedral? You're f—in' nuts, man. Churches are swarming with vagrants. You want some homeless guy to get his grimy paws on our twenty thousand? What if some priest finds it? They're the greediest of all. We can kiss our sweet payday goodbye."

"No, dude. It's brilliant. Last place anyone would look. I scoped it out. An entry fee weeds out the homeless. There's a statue of Mary with a hollow pedestal. We're gone three, four days tops. We make the drop with Raphael and we're back with another twenty grand. Sweet Mother Mary, dude."

"When do you suggest we do this, Ace?"

"The cathedral is always packed with tourists except first thing when it opens and again before it closes. We do it in the morning."

"After breakfast, man, okay?"

"Do you one better. You stay here with the drugs and I plant the money. Less conspicuous. That way, we keep the coke and cash separate."

"And I get breakfast."

The sound of loud, head-banging music stirred Beatrice. She lifted her head to see her roommate scramble to reinsert a headphone cord into her phone. The sterile room was awash with light. Beatrice's stomach growled for food.

After showering, Beatrice made her way to the dining room. She put down her tray at a table, ignoring the hulk of a guy in a torn Megadeth T-shirt seated at the opposite end. He seemed too eager for a conversation. As she drank her coffee, she tried to piece together the dream fragments. Her subconscious had been on overload since she ran away from home. For two months she had suffered a regular barrage of nightmares. She understood why.

Her life had been on a downward spiral for more than a year—the death of her mother, her father's bouts of depression and bursts of anger, news of Joost's engagement, then the wedding itself. She didn't mean to get drunk at the reception, or maybe she did. Humiliation came when she made a spectacle of herself on the dance floor. At one point, she bumped into Liv, nearly toppling the Norwegian princess onto her perfect ass. After saving his bride, Joost led Beatrice outside with a firm hand and an even firmer message. "I care for you, Bea, but I don't recognize you anymore. Go home. You're drunk."

Drugs and alcohol provided an escape from Beatrice's dead-end life. She didn't intend to steal from her father. The first time was simple, a fifty-euro note slipped from the cash register at the end of the day to pay for a fix. She planned to pay her father back. But when the cash wasn't missed, she took more. Whenever her conscience stirred, she told herself that she deserved the money as payback for having to endure her father's mood swings and settle for a life she never wanted—making cakes for other people's happy lives. But when the bakery went into the red, her father brought in an auditor. The rat-eyed codger with yellow teeth and foul breath discovered the ongoing thievery.

"Quid pro quo, young woman." He promised to keep her secret in exchange for sex. "You're really in no position to argue. An addict and a thief."

She had never felt so degraded. She fled. For all she knew, her father filed a complaint with the police. The random train she boarded terminated at Antwerp Central station. *Fine a place as any…for now*, she said to herself as she stood with her suitcase under the vast dome of the station's grand entrance hall. *Antwerp's big enough for me to disappear*. However, if she ever scraped together enough money, she'd escape to Italy or even America.

As Beatrice slathered the dense breakfast bread with butter, she thought back to the prior night's dream—drug money hidden in the cathedral. Such a windfall would be a wish come true. She could pay back her father with interest and still have enough money left for a new life. She'd been considering design school. Antwerp was full of them.

"Twenty thousand euros," she muttered aloud. "Sure would answer my prayers. Sweet Mother Mary, indeed."

As Beatrice chuckled aloud about her fantasy, she noticed the hulk with whom she shared the table flinch before glaring at her with a quizzical look on his face. He seemed surprised, angry—dangerous. Beatrice figured she might encounter a loony or two in the hostel. As he began to address her, she took advantage of the passing hostel proprietor.

Beatrice rose from the table with her tray. "Fantastic hostel," she said to the smiling Asian woman. "Bed and shower are awesome. Breakfast's bad-ass fine."

The woman grinned. "You give good review on Internet."

"Sure thing. Can I walk with you?" Time on the streets had taught Beatrice the art of extricating herself from unsavory characters.

Beatrice exited the hostel's front door, abruptly changing direction when she spotted two blue-uniformed police officers heading toward her. After several casual paces, she glanced over her shoulder. She exhaled a sigh of relief. Instead of following her, the officers marched into the hostel. Even that move, however, was troubling. What if they were there for her? She'd planned to return to the hostel for the night if the rain didn't let up. The proprietor said she'd save a bed.

Beatrice couldn't worry about that. She continued on a path that took her into the heart of the old city. She clung to the buildings to keep dry. Antwerp had always been the magical place where her parents brought her for holiday shopping and cultural events, before her mother fell ill. But besides those fond childhood memories, she never really knew the city.

As she wandered the streets as a homeless woman, she admired Antwerp's vitality—chic avenues with designer stores, pedestrian zones of cheap trinkets and mediocre food, and finer restaurants with well-dressed clientele. And always a steady stream of eager-eyed tourists filled in around the edges.

The sixteenth-century Grote Markt, more triangular than square, rivaled that of Brussels, a city that her parents called too dirty, too

French. Fairy-tale guildhalls with glistening gold statues atop Flemish gables ringed the plaza dominated by a Renaissance-inspired town hall. In front of the flag-draped town hall, a verdigris statue depicted the city's mythical origins. The work included mermaids and water-spouting creatures including a fish, sea lion, turtle, and dragon. On rocks above this menagerie, a Roman hero was tossing the severed hand of an evil giant. The statue's vivid features had wormed their way into more than a few of Beatrice's recent nightmares.

Antwerp embraced artistry and design with the same passion that Beatrice imagined flourished in Florence and New York. The commercial city provided a nurturing home to Rubens, Van Dyck, and many other painters and sculptors. Unlike Rembrandt, who died a pauper in Amsterdam, Rubens was one of the wealthiest artists of his time. If Beatrice could live her life over again, she'd be an artist, or at least a designer of furniture, fashion, or….It didn't matter. It was mere fantasy anyway, unlikely to ever come true.

She didn't quite know how it happened, but Beatrice found herself in front of the cathedral. The magnificent Gothic structure was six hundred years old. Its spire, the tallest in the Low Countries, soared to a height of more than four hundred feet. Napoleon compared its delicate ornamentation to fine lace. Had her dream drawn Beatrice there, or was it simply habit? While living on the streets, she had spent several afternoons inside the mighty cathedral to kill time and squelch her boredom. The entry fee wasn't a deterrent; she learned to piggyback her way inside for free with large groups.

Inside the cathedral, she made her way to her favorite spot. Located on the north aisle, the Mary chapel was shrouded in shadow. Beatrice could spend time there without drawing any notice. Unlike the church's other cavernous spaces, the Mary chapel was intimate, its scale human. At its entrance stood a simple fourteenth-century marble statue of Madonna and Child. Despite the glorious masterpieces of Rubens that adorned the cathedral, this was Beatrice's favorite piece. Baby Jesus caresses his mother's cheek, playfully, lovingly. Mary looks on with motherly affection. *The statue's power,* Beatrice thought, *is its simple beauty and human touch. It could represent any mother and child.* The statue made her think of her own mother. Guilt nagged at Beatrice for the way she blamed her mother's illness for her own failed life. She had said some vile things. But regret came too late; her mother was dead.

Beatrice chose a seat nearest the outer wall. She placed her rucksack and shoulder bag on the straight-backed chair beside her. She stared ahead at a trough of offertory candles at the front of the chapel. It was still early in the day, but several flames already flickered with the prayers of the faithful or, maybe, merely the dreams and pleas of desperate souls like herself. During her frequent visits, Beatrice had lit candles for her parents. She sometimes wondered, however, if skipping the one-euro fee meant her prayers languished in the cold, stale air of the cathedral.

Behind the flickering candles stood a marble altar decorated with white granite columns and silver candlesticks. Another, more elaborate statue of the Madonna and Child presided in a raised arched alcove behind the altar. Marble urns filled with roses, statice, and baby's-breath sat as tributes on each side. A silk gown of emerald green adorned the statue of painted wood, but what made this Madonna less human were the golden crown and scepter.

When Beatrice closed her eyes, her thoughts returned to the prior night. As the last dream bloomed again in her head, its seeds became clear—the men's conversation echoed the world of drugs, money, and thievery into which she had descended. Twenty thousand euros promised salvation, a chance to redeem herself with her father, make amends to all she'd hurt. But the two drug dealers—what was her connection to them? After some consideration, she decided they were voices of her guilty conscience. And try as she might, she couldn't shake their dialogue. *It all seemed so real.*

She laughed at herself for even considering it. Hell, the church contained dozens of statues of the Virgin Mary. What made her think this was the one, that is, if the money were even real? She rose from the chair but hesitated. *Silly, stupid girl.* But a voice from within, as soft, kind, and faint as her own mother's, told her to proceed.

Beatrice waited until a middle-aged couple exited the chapel before approaching the altar. Heat from the prayer candles warmed her face, a contrast to the cool ambient air. With another glance around the chapel, she stepped over the velvet rope that cordoned off the altar. The sweet scent of roses mixed with incense and candle wax. *What if I'm caught?* She started to perspire. Again she looked over her shoulder to ensure that she was alone. She inched behind the altar and gazed up at the Virgin Mary. Impulsively, she thrust her hand behind the statue's pedestal—nothing. On tiptoe, she reached up and under the ornate green gown. She patted the area on one side, then the other. A massive silver candlestick teetered. She held her breath until it steadied. She reached farther back—nothing but cold plaster.

Stupid fool! Look at you. How pitiful. Self-recrimination repeated in her head as she climbed down from the altar.

Returning to the trough of candles, she began to sob. She didn't know why. Perhaps she missed her mother; perhaps she realized her folly. A silly dream had provoked this foolish escapade, raising her hopes then dashing them again. It was the same kind of nonsense—childish fantasy—that had ended in disappointment with Joost. After sitting down to compose herself, Beatrice felt compelled to escape the cathedral.

She gathered her belongings. As she made her way out of the chapel, the sun broke through the stormy sky, sending a beam of intense light through a high window. The brilliant ray fell upon the simple marble statue she most admired. Mary's face lit up, her expression kind, sympathetic. Instinctively, Beatrice crouched down. She reached behind the pedestal, fiddling with the wooden panel. She gasped at the touch of plastic. Tugging the plastic sack from its hiding place, she felt the presence of someone looming over her.

The stern voice spoke before Beatrice had a chance to turn. "Young woman, *please.*" Spinning around, she gazed up to find a fat, white-haired priest. His black robe rested on top of his sandals. A crucifix dangled from a chain around his neck. "This isn't a garbage dump."

"I…I'm sorry. B…but it's not—"

His cold glare silenced her. "I've seen you before. Your entry ticket, please."

"Oh! Okay." She began to rummage through her bag.

The priest thrust his finger toward the pedestal. "First, your trash."

In a flash, Beatrice grabbed the plastic sack. Her heart raced when she felt the wad of cash inside. "Sorry, father, but I have to run." She lifted herself up and dashed toward the door leaving the priest muttering curses and shaking his head.

As she hurried out the front door, a well-dressed man marching into the cathedral caught her attention. Perhaps he reminded her of Joost. Good-looking, this dark-haired man also wore his hair slicked back. His eyes were the same shade of blue and just as intense as those of her friend. But it was the man's companion who sparked her thoughts. She'd seen the droopy-eyed guy before. *But where?* She got her answer when he moved from behind a group of Chinese tourists. *That T-shirt!* It was the shaggy-haired stoner in the Megadeth shirt from the hostel—the guy at the breakfast table. He didn't strike her as the cathedral type. Then again, she wasn't the church type either.

She hurried her pace, then gasped. *Oh, Beatrice, what have you done?* It all fit. The plastic sack in her shoulder bag proved that the money and now the two disembodied voices obviously weren't dreams. Her careless comments at breakfast about the money explained the piercing look the stoner had shot her. *He knows I know.* She glanced back. The two men had disappeared inside the cathedral.

She figured she only had a matter of minutes, if not seconds, before the men discovered their loss. If she was lucky, the pedantic priest would delay them. But then, they'd be after her, not stopping until they caught her. Nobody let twenty grand get away without a fight. The hulk in the Megadeth shirt knew her face and the intense guy looked smart enough to ask the chubby priest if he'd seen someone matching her description. She had to get far away—fast.

Beatrice ran across the square to the lane leading to Oude Koornmarkt Straat. Cheap restaurants with outdoor seating usually drew a crowd. But she found the street virtually deserted. A heavy downpour gave her an excuse to sprint without suspicion. She ran toward the river, turning left onto Hoogstraat. Even in the rain, tourists couldn't resist the cluster of shops along the pedestrian zone. Hoogstraat led into Kloosterstraat, which always bustled with antique hunters and artsy types. She could blend in. If she felt herself being followed, she could duck into one of the many secondhand stores.

The rain intensified, forcing Beatrice to stop under an awning. She hadn't really searched the sack. What if it wasn't cash? Across the street she spotted a restaurant. Vines covered the signs on both faces of the corner building. Green awnings provided protection from the rain to patrons seated at colorful metal tables along an L-shaped terrace. The crowded café would give her cover as well as a chance to think.

Once inside, she found the restaurant warm, folksy, and, best of all, dim. She walked past the long bar to an area decorated with bookshelves, plush chairs, and a sofa. She nodded to a young headphone-wearing woman who sipped coffee while staring at her computer screen. A black and white terrier curled up at her feet.

Beatrice made her way to the ladies toilet, locking the door behind her. At the sink, her fingers twitched as she opened her shoulder bag and pulled out the plastic sack. Her heart raced. She opened the sack slowly. Rolled up with rubber bands was more money than she'd ever seen. Taking deep breaths, she counted it—twenty thousand euros. *Sweet Mother Mary.*

Her problems were over. *Or, have they just begun?*

After repacking the cash, she washed her hands and splashed water on her face. She did up her hair and added what little makeup she possessed to alter her appearance. But she needed a better plan. *Joost,* she thought, *he always has solutions.* But after the scene at his wedding, she wasn't sure he wanted to talk to her. Besides, he'd probably consider the matter unsavory, something in which an up-and-coming lawyer shouldn't get involved. No, she was alone. If she found herself in trouble, she couldn't even go to the police. They'd never believe a homeless addict and thief.

Inside the restaurant, Beatrice sank into a plush chair. She ordered a coffee. Voices from outside the open window caught her attention. Two men were having a grand time with a waitress. Their laughter and frivolity were stark and enviable contrasts to her agitated state of mind. Curious, she peered at them. The two men seated at a red metal table were ruggedly handsome with good Flemish features—light hair, prominent noses, strong chins, and rectangular faces. They could be father and son, two brothers, or merely close friends. The younger man was about her age and the other older, but she couldn't tell by how much. They looked healthy and strong—tans, thick muscles, and big hands—men who made their living outdoors.

"Not that I'm tired of you two salty dogs," the server said, "but haven't you stayed in Antwerp longer than usual? You forget your old motto about the rolling stone?"

The older fellow laughed. "No moss for us. We've got to shove off tonight before the dock keeper locks up the *Sagittarius*."

"Seems he likes to get paid. Imagine that," added the younger one before taking a large gulp of beer.

The server put her hand on her hip. "And so do I. Imagine that! Sounds like I better wait here till you pay your bill." But it was all for fun as she leaned over and kissed each man on his cheek.

From their conversation, Beatrice learned that the men operated a houseboat. They chartered it for tourists who wanted a unique European holiday. Belgium, in fact, had more than fifteen hundred miles of navigable waterways. A series of rivers and canals connected Antwerp to Brussels and Liège. Even more options within the nearby Netherlands offered endless cruising adventures. The men had to move their boat to Brussels to collect a rich American couple and a hefty fee. The pickup was three days away. Until they got paid, they didn't have enough cash to cover dock fees in either Antwerp or Brussels. Instead of a journey that normally took less than a day, they planned to meander through the Belgian waterways, docking only where there were no fees.

The older guy wrapped his arm around the server's waist and pulled her close. "We still need a cook. How about you, sweet cheeks?"

"That a proposal?"

"Sure, if you can cook too."

"And be stuck on a boat with you two? A deer would fare better in a wolves' lair."

The American clients sounded pampered. The men explained that the couple had a full domestic staff back at their estate in the Hamptons. A holiday touring Europe's canals on a houseboat was already "roughing it." They demanded a cook.

Beatrice saw an opening, a chance to slip out of Antwerp undercover. Megadeth and his slick buddy would watch the train station, but they'd never think of looking toward the river. Three days on a houseboat would give her time to think, make plans. Once she reached Brussels safely, she could ditch her saviors.

Beatrice poked her head out the window. "Couldn't help overhearing. If you're serious about needing a cook, you've found your girl. Bake too. Boy, can I bake."

The younger man stood. Beatrice thought she'd never seen such a beautiful smile and deep green eyes. "Looks like it's our lucky day. I'm Sebastian. This here's Max. On the water, we're known as the Vervloet cousins. And what's the name of our new chief cook and bottle washer?"

The answer came to her in a split second, the same alias she'd used at the hostel. "Liv, Liv Peeters."

Beatrice had to be at the dock before ten o'clock that night. The Vervloet cousins intended to steal away after dark. Their route would take them up the Scheldt River. At the confluence with the Rupel, they'd enter the Wintam lock for the twenty-eight-kilometer journey up the canal and into central Brussels. Max and Sebastian gave her the option of joining them in Brussels during the layover, but she told them no. In retrospect, perhaps her tone sounded a bit desperate. The cousins exchanged a look but shook it off. They seemed thrilled at finding a cook. In setting a rendezvous time later that day, the cousins assumed that their new cook needed to collect more things and inform family of the month-long, multinational work assignment. Silence kept Beatrice's lies to a minimum.

That evening, when Beatrice reached the well-lit dock, she voiced a spontaneous, "Wow!"

Instead of a modern houseboat that resembled the cabin cruisers and fiberglass yachts she saw cruising local rivers, the boat belonging to the Vervloet cousins was an old-fashioned beauty. The wooden vessel was more reminiscent of the long canal boats she'd seen on a visit to Amsterdam although this one was shorter, stubbier. The part of the hull at and below the waterline was lacquered black. Just above, three freshly painted stripes ringed the hull—cobalt blue, vermilion, and white. The cabin, boathouse, and deck itself were polished in a pecan stain to a brilliant sheen. Wooden railings and trim were stained a dark, glossy finish while porthole casings and other hardware were accented in brushed nickel.

This, Beatrice thought, was a museum piece, a boat fit for prime ministers, presidents, kings, and pampered Americans from Long Island. She could only imagine the countless hours Sebastian and Max had spent polishing it up in anticipation of the finicky, deep-pocketed couple.

The older cousin, Max, jumped from the boat onto the dock. He was tall and broad-shouldered with crinkles around his dark eyes. He smelled masculine, musky. When he put his large hand on her back, she felt its warmth through her cotton shirt. "Evening, Liv. Welcome to the *Sagittarius*. She's a real beaut, isn't she?"

"Bad-ass fine," she replied, before catching her profanity. "I mean, gorgeous, absolutely gorgeous. Never seen anything like it."

Max squared his shoulders. She could see the pride on his face. "Vintage, don't you know. Not many of these babies left. Sebastian and I sank all we had into her. That's why we charge a premium. Full service, five-star cruising." He grabbed her backpack and shoulder bag. "Now scamper aboard, galley master."

On board, Max explained the plan. Sebastian had gone to the dock office to see the night manager. He was pretending to settle their account to clear the way for a morning departure. He intended to boast about a pricey charter up to Amsterdam and through the Frisian Islands. In reality, they were heading in the opposite direction. Max needed only to wait for Sebastian's text saying that he'd begun his tactical diversion before casting off.

"When presented with the bill, he'll raise bloody hell. Pound on the table, stomp on the floor. He'll demand an adjustment, insist the manager call the big boss at home. By the time he's through with his shenanigans, we'll be long gone. He'll make some excuse to get away. We'll pick him up on the other side of the city."

While they waited for Sebastian at a deserted dock on the other side of Antwerp, Max gave Beatrice a tour. The prow housed the cousins' cabin—twin beds, a reading chair, and an antique wooden table that opened into a desk. The bookcase above a dresser was a catchall for liquor bottles, books, candles, and glassware. Maps and nautical instruments filled the walls. A door led to a small toilet and sink. Moving aft was a narrow hall. A bathroom with modern conveniences and vintage décor occupied the port side. Beatrice's sleeping quarters were starboard. Her cabin was larger than she'd imagined, the décor charming, romantic. Max explained that some clients, those who didn't require a cook, used the cabin for extra guests. Beatrice couldn't stop staring at the warm, plush four-poster bed.

Aft of Beatrice's cabin and up a few steps was the galley. With cherrywood cabinets and stainless-steel appliances, it resembled the kitchen of a posh flat. There was a fully stocked wine chiller and a pantry loaded with cookware and staples. Beatrice wouldn't have any trouble preparing haute cuisine. Aft of the galley was the lounge. The room contained a leather sofa and matching chairs, burl-wood dining table, well-stocked bar, and flat-screen TV. The brass telescope, Max pointed out, could be moved up to the sundeck for stargazing.

"Wow!" Beatrice exclaimed when Max opened the door to the suite spanning the entire stern. The bedroom and adjoining bath were as luxurious as the five-star hotels she saw on television.

Hearing footsteps on the dock and then a thump, Beatrice jumped.

"Calm yourself, Liv. That's only Sebastian. I can tell his flat feet anywhere."

Up on the deck, they found the younger cousin throwing back a bottle of beer. Looking pleased with himself, he flashed a smile and offered his raised palm to Max for a victory slap. "I bellowed so loud, Chubs didn't know what hit him. Hell, I scared myself. As he was getting the dock boss on the phone, I told him I needed the toilet. He probably thinks I had a stroke in there." Sebastian laughed, slapping Beatrice on the arm. "Oh, sorry."

"No worries."

In this frenzied state, Sebastian was even more handsome than before. His bronzed brow glistened with sweat. Beneath his jeans and white T-shirt, taut muscles flexed. He fanned himself with a red and blue checked shirt that he'd taken off in a bid to cool down.

"You boys must be starving from all your heroics. How about I whip up some dinner?" The cousins looked at each other, grinning as if they hit it rich.

"Hell, yes," Sebastian said.

"I'll open a bottle of wine," added Max.

After dinner, Max pushed himself from the table. He leaned backward, his hands patting his stomach. "Shoulda charged the Americans more."

Beatrice had used what she found in the galley to prepare North Sea salmon with scalloped potatoes. Crème brûlée with creamy orange custard drew sighs of orgasmic delight from the cousins. As Beatrice basked in their praise, she began to feel pangs of guilt for misleading them. What would they think of her after she abandoned them in Brussels?

The cousins moved from coffee to whiskey. Beatrice did too.

After a few rounds, Max turned to Sebastian. "Meant to ask you, what the hell took you so long to launch your dramatic scene with Chubs? Liv and I waited for your all-clear text for over thirty minutes."

Sebastian slapped Max's shoulder. "One doesn't rush fine acting." He doubled over with laughter. "Actually," he added after composing himself, "I had to wait. Another guy was bending Chubs' ear. Intense, too. Looking for some girl named Beatrice."

Beatrice's whiskey glass stopped at her lips. "What did he look like?"

Sebastian shrugged. "Fancy dresser. Intense, like I said. Slicked back hair, blue eyes. Why you ask?"

"Just wondering, that's all." But Beatrice's stomach soured at the image of Megadeth's slick companion. How had the druggies discovered her name so fast? She used an alias at the hostel. But not on the street. *That's it.* Some homeless guy gave her up for a joint and bottle of gin. "He alone?"

"Yep. Gave Chubs his card. Told him to call if he saw her. Promised a reward."

Max stared at Beatrice as if his mind were churning with questions. He turned to his cousin. "This guy, he say why he was looking for her?"

Sebastian shook his head. "Nope. Personal matter, that's all. Gave me the cold shoulder when he heard we were shoving off."

Beatrice pretended to be unfazed by the information but felt Max's dark eyes study her. *Careful, Bea, don't give yourself away.*

"Hell, Liv," Sebastian added. "If Maxie and I weren't so desperate for a cook, I'd be wonderin' where you came from."

Max nodded. "You did drop into our lives like a miracle, that's for sure." She detected the uncertainty in his voice. Then he clanked his glass against hers and grinned. "But shit, you cook like an angel. I'm not about to ask questions I don't want the answer to."

They all laughed, but Beatrice wasn't so sure her cover was safe. That night she lay awake in her cabin. *What have I gotten myself into?* Could she outrun the drug dealers? Had she brought danger to the Vervloet cousins? A more ominous thought popped into her head. *Can I trust Sebastian and Max?*

Nothing more was said of the intense dock inquisitor or the mysterious Beatrice. Over the course of the next two days, Beatrice cooked breakfast, lunch, and dinner for the cousins. Their heavy drinking gave cover to her own indulgences. They smoked the occasional joint and passed it to her. She learned that Sebastian's parents had died in a car accident when he was a child. Max's father, a sailor on a merchant ship, had abandoned his family before the orphaned Sebastian went to live with his aunt and cousin. Max, more than a decade older, was the father Sebastian never had. The love and respect shared by the two men were unmistakable. Their devotion to each other touched Beatrice.

She found life on the water enchanting, simpler, fun. She tried to keep a low profile, but the *Sagittarius* drew admirers wherever they went. Everyone on the river and in the small villages at which they docked had a smile and hearty greeting for the Vervloet cousins. The work and camaraderie filled her with satisfaction. She felt purposeful, appreciated, even loved. There was also an unexpected side effect. Her craving for cocaine and binge drinking diminished.

Despite her happiness, Beatrice cautioned herself about becoming too attached to Max and Sebastian. She fought urges to become emotionally involved. The opportunity for sex was there with each cousin. She was certain that she simply needed to show a little interest. But such an intimate entanglement risked hurting the sweet guys even more. They'd hate her enough when she abandoned them in Brussels.

After a lovely evening bundled in blankets on the upper deck stargazing and drinking wine, Sebastian called it a night. "Gotta get some rest. Tomorrow's the end of our holiday. We herald the arrival of Queen Donna and King Stephen of Sagaponack."

"Just in the nick of time. Somebody's gotta pay for our high living," Max said before turning to Beatrice, his glass hoisted. "Speaking of high living, a toast to the best chef this side of the Rhine. Livvy, our miracle angel, you made two men very happy—and fat," he added, patting his stomach.

After the toast, each man kissed her on the cheek and Sebastian headed below deck. As was his custom, Max stayed up to *keep watch*, as he liked to say. He would sit at the wheel with a cigarette and whiskey—his quiet time to commune with his beloved boat.

Max put his arm around Beatrice and kissed her cheek. "Stay with me, Liv."

Her heart told her to remain, but her head said no. After all of his kindness and generosity, she didn't want to start something she had no intention of seeing through. "I'd love to," she replied with a forced smile, "but we've got a big day tomorrow. Need my rest." She sensed disappointment, his hurt feelings, as she extracted herself from his embrace.

Alone in her cabin, Beatrice felt great anguish. She was fond of Max and Sebastian, very fond. "But it's not Beatrice Sterk they love," she said, sobbing into her pillow. "It's Liv Peeters." She reached into her rucksack for what remained of the vodka and drank herself to sleep.

"Brussels, ahoy!" Max shouted from the wheelhouse.

Beatrice finished tidying the galley and the forward cabins. She pulled the list of provisions needs off the refrigerator. After reviewing it, she tucked it into her jeans pocket with the money Max had given her for the purchase. She hated herself for what she was about to do. But she was in danger, and as long as she stayed with them, so were the cousins.

Looking dashing in dress khakis and a blue polo, Sebastian popped his head into the galley. "Need a strapping guy?"

Beatrice ruffled his hair. "Always. What do you have in mind?"

"To help cart the supplies. But the offer's open to other things," he added with a suggestive wink.

She threw a galley towel at him. "Scram, you water rat! What I can't carry I'll have delivered."

Beatrice planned to order the provisions and have them delivered to the boat. She didn't want her disappearance to be a complete disaster for the cousins. They still needed to feed their clients. They wouldn't miss her until later that evening, when she didn't show up for the scheduled departure. The note she planned to leave in her cabin would offer an explanation of her sudden disappearance—some lame excuse about a sick fictitious grandmother.

She waited for the cousins to visit the dock master before collecting her belongings and making her escape.

After ordering and arranging the delivery of provisions, Beatrice wandered through Brussels. A liquor store made an all-too-familiar appeal. After a few moments of deliberation and even an initial walk-by, she retraced her steps and succumbed. A return to the bottle and other comforts, she figured, would cure the anticipated onset of depression. After a few swigs of vodka, she made her way to the city center. She didn't know the old city, but she figured cocaine wouldn't be hard to score.

To her surprise, Brussels had assumed a carnival atmosphere. Revelers in medieval costumes filled the streets. Approaching the Grand Place, she came upon a procession of horses mounted by riders dressed as knights with swords and pennants. Maidens in colorful dresses with dashing consorts sat in open carriages. It was the stuff of fairy tales.

Beatrice sidled up to an English tourist who was watching the spectacle with his family. "What's all this?"

"Something called the Ommegang, a parade and pageant to celebrate some legend. It's great for the kids," he added, ruffling the hair of two toddlers huddling before him.

She continued her walk but froze in her tracks. *Impossible! What shitty luck.* At the entrance to the Grand Place, where gabled buildings narrowed the walking path, stood the two druggies from Antwerp. They were scanning the faces of the crowd entering and exiting the Grand Place.

Beatrice panicked. The money was no longer important. She'd already decided that. Three days on the houseboat had shown her that she could make an honest living as a chef. She knew she couldn't merely give back the money. She knew too much for the drug dealers to let her go. Backtracking to the English tourist, she asked to use his phone. His wife cast her a suspicious look, elbowing her husband and shaking her head. But the husband reached into his pocket and handed Beatrice his phone.

She punched in the number. After three rings, there was an answer. "Joost?"

"Beatrice? Where are you? Your father and I've been searching for you everywhere." His voice was firm but not harsh.

"You have?"

"You've had us all crazed."

"I bet. Guessing Father's got the police out to arrest me."

"Huh, arrest? Oh, the missing money. Sure he was mad, Bea. He had every right to be. But he doesn't care about that anymore. He even slugged that rodent-faced auditor in the gut when he mentioned the police. Blames himself. He just wants his daughter back. He loves you, Bea. Heck, he's been looking for you in Brussels, Bruges, and Ghent."

"Oh, the poor man."

"Liv and I've been scouring Antwerp, Rotterdam, and Amsterdam. I even tracked you to a hostel. The grinning Asian woman remembered you. Said two other guys were looking for you too. I visited the train station and docks."

"The docks?" *So it was Joost, not the slick drug dealer, that Sebastian saw in the dock manager's office.*

"Where are you?"

"Brussels. Joost, I'm in trouble."

"I'm coming to get you."

"Don't you want to know—"

"That can wait. You know the church in the Grand Sablon?"

"How could I forget?" Joost's choice of that church for a rendezvous was no coincidence. During the summer after high school, Beatrice and Joost had traveled to Brussels for a last hurrah before he went off to university. Beatrice fell in love with the fifteenth-century church that graced the Grand Sablon. After telling Joost it was where she wanted to have her wedding, she pulled him into a pew. The two kissed until a priest suggested they take their passion outside.

"I'll get there as soon as I can. An hour tops if the motorway's clear."

Avoiding the two druggies, Beatrice made her way through the city to the Grand Sablon. She used the crowds of tourists and costumed parade-goers as cover. Inside the church, a wave of nostalgia hit her. She glanced under the ornate wooden pulpit to the pew where she and Joost had kissed. *Oh, how our lives have changed in seven years.* Perhaps the past three days with Max and Sebastian changed her most of all. Before sitting in the pew where she'd wait for Joost, Beatrice approached the statue of the Virgin Mary. She lit candles for her parents and the Vervloet cousins, and one for herself. The same sweet, kind voice that had spoken to her in the Antwerp cathedral spoke again. "Listen to your heart, Beatrice."

An hour seemed like an eternity, but Joost finally arrived. Her hero was as handsome as the day they had visited the church. They embraced like the old friends they were. Beatrice apologized again for her behavior at the wedding, but Joost told her not to give it another thought. He knew it was the drugs and alcohol. He loved her—as a

STUFF OF DREAMS

friend. He and Liv were prepared to help her in any way they could.

Sitting together with clasped hands, Beatrice relayed her story and Joost listened, nodding as Beatrice described the two drug dealers. He knew of them, Raphael too. They were well-known criminals in Belgium. He'd come across their names in his work defending young offenders. Belgian authorities would welcome any help to put them away.

Beatrice reached into her rucksack and handed over the money. "You'll know what to do with this."

Joost expressed confidence that they'd be arrested in a matter of days. The money and her testimony could help convict them. "Might even be a reward."

"Give it to Father. Tell him I love him. I'll call when I can."

Joost looked confused. "But?"

Beatrice grinned. "But right now, I can't mess up my best chance for a fabulous life."

Joost tilted his head. "Seriously?"

"Yep, the stuff of dreams."

Joost's blue eyes looked at her with affection before he kissed her on the cheek.

At the church door, Beatrice paused to look over her shoulder. A tear welled in her eye as her heart bid farewell to Joost and her old life. She wasn't so much sad as satisfied—she'd found her way. She turned into the sunshine of the Grand Sablon. She didn't know whether she had a chance with Max or Sebastian. But she was willing to give it a try. Let love flourish where it may.

Beatrice dropped the vodka bottle into a trash bin. "Sweet Mother Mary," she said before taking a deep breath and sprinting back to the dock and the Vervloet cousins.

A Belgian Photo Assortment

*From the author's private collection
taken between December 2013 and December 2015*

Grand Place, Brussels

Grand Place, Brussels

Town Hall, Brussels

Church of Saint Catherine, Brussels

Market Square with Menin Gate Memorial, Ieper/Ypres

City Hall of Antwerp

Essex Farm Cemetery, Ieper

Brabo Fountain, Grote Markt, Antwerp

Cathedral of Our Lady, Antwerp

Canal, Bruges

*Monument Depicting the Legend of Beatrijs Soetkens,
Church of Our Blessed Lady of the Sablon, Brussels*

Canal, Bruges

Belfry of Bruges

Church of Saint-Gilles and Parvis, Brussels

Parvis de Saint–Gilles, Brussels

Saint-Gilles Town Hall and Market, Brussels

Chocolate Shop Window Display, Antwerp

Church of Our Blessed Lady of the Sablon, Brussels

Petit Sablon, Brussels

Arcades du Cinquantenaire, Brussels

In Bruges...Again

"Plenty to see and do, that's for sure."

Jack Ramsey sat in his underwear on a rented sofa in his bright, modern apartment, speaking to his mother's video image on his computer screen. Three years prior, when he announced his transfer to Belgium, June had insisted on weekly Skype sessions. Jack didn't know if it was because his mother wanted to keep a close eye on her boy or feared he'd forget her. Brussels was seven time zones and a world away from her suburban Milwaukee home. He didn't discount loneliness. Jack's father had died four years earlier, less than twelve months before Jack's European transfer, and June's only other child, an older son, lived ninety miles south, in Chicago.

"Plenty to see right here in Brussels. The Grand Place, Atomium, Mannequin Pis—"

"That cute little naked boy who pees all the time?" June interrupted with a chuckle. "Lydia mentioned him at coffee. Says he needs senior diapers more than she does."

Jack laughed. He was happy to see his mom so excited about her upcoming visit. Her face glowed when she spoke about her first trip "outta the good ole U.S. of A.," though Jack reminded her that, technically, Canada was a foreign country. His father Ed had driven the family to Manitoba every year for a camping holiday "to toughen up his boys" with fishing, hunting, and a number of other hardy outdoor activities that young Jack loathed. It was on one such trip that his father decided that little Johnny should be called Jack. "It's a more manly name, God damn it, June," Ed said to end his wife's objections.

"We'll see the peeing boy, Mom. But I warn you, he's not that impressive."

"Most men aren't, Jack, believe you me." June's eyes sparkled as her fair Irish skin took on the faintest blush. After becoming a widow, she had dated occasionally, doing so only after Jack's prodding. "What about Bruges?" she added, as if sparked by a recollection. "Definitely Bruges. 'Don't miss Bruges,' Dolores said. You know Dolores, been everywhere, done everything. It's not worth visiting unless she's seen it." In the weekly Skype sessions, June often quoted her Starbucks lady friends, as she called them.

Jack swallowed hard. "Bruges?"

"Why that look, Jackaroo?"

Sometimes Jack hated technology. He preferred the days before video when he could multitask during one of his mother's marathon phone calls, interjecting the occasional "uh-huh," "yeah," "yep," and "really" to keep her going.

"What look? I don't have a look. Do I?"

"I'm your mother. That crooked smile and tense jaw always give you away. Isn't Bruges a nice place?"

"It's not that." Jack gazed at his image, a small square in the corner of his computer screen. He forced his lips straight and tried to relax his jaw. "Bruges is great. A must-see, for sure."

"Then what is it?"

"Er…nothing."

Her bluish-gray eyes glared at him. "Jackaroo?"

He sighed. She didn't have to tell him that, as his mother, she could read his face better than anyone. Her tone implied it. "Everyone who visits wants to go," he replied. "I've been to Bruges so many times I could give tours in my sleep."

The excitement vanished from June's face. "Well…we don't have to go…not if you don't want. What does Dolores know, anyway? I'm just happy to see you."

His mother assumed an expression Jack had witnessed his entire life—wide eyes, raised eyebrows, and a pursed-lipped smile. It was the same face absent wrinkles when little Jacky explained that his third grade art project wasn't a doily but an Easter bonnet he expected her to wear to mass. Or the time he refused to take her best friend's daughter to the prom, lying about having to cover an open shift at his drugstore job. June's stilted reaction was exactly the same when he broke the news of his expat assignment. Like most mothers, June hid her disappointment and concern behind a mask of unconditional love. That same look never failed to stir Jack's guilt.

"Can't come all this way and not see Bruges."

"Just put me on a bus. There must be a bus."

Jack hid his thoughts behind gritted teeth and a closed-mouth smile. *Sure, send my seventy-year-old mother on a bus. That'll play well with the coffee ladies.* "We're going to Bruges and that's that…*together*. You'll have the best tour guide in town," he added with a wink. "There's a train. Or, I can drive."

The glow returned to June's face. "You decide, honey. I leave that to you."

"We've got a few weeks yet," he said, noticing a change in her expression, a desire to add something more. "And?"

Her gaze shifted away from the camera. "And what?"

"There's more you want to say. I see it in your face. I'm your son, remember? Your favorite one at that."

June grinned. The glint in her eye informed him that he'd hit the mark. "Okay, Jackaroo. Just wondering if I'll get to meet your friends, that's all."

"Sure, sure. You'll meet them." He sensed she was fishing for more.

"Maybe a…a special someone?"

And there it was. "Oh, Mom."

"Oh Mom what? Your poor little ole mother sits here in Milwaukee worrying about her boy. It's not okay for me to want to see you happy? Bet there's lots of nice Belgians who'd want to snag a good-looking, successful American banker."

"Sure, sure, lots of green-card seekers, gold diggers, and cat ladies have thrown themselves at me." He usually found humor a good weapon to deflect this line of questioning. But June didn't crack a smile. Her eyes held firm. Jack relented; he shook his head. "No, there's no special someone…yet. Too busy with work. Besides, expats hang out as a group. Lots of my friends are single." Jack's muscles tensed. Even he knew that he sounded desperate, defensive. But, he was on high alert. A Skype session was neither the time nor place to talk to his mother about his love life. He didn't know what the right time or place looked like, but this wasn't it. Four thousand miles separated them, and a two-week shared holiday loomed in their near future.

Adopting another tactic, Jack changed the subject. "Pack sensible shoes and comfortable clothes. You know, jeans, sweatshirts…"

"Yes, honey, I made my list. Oh, oh, what about a hair dryer?"

"I bought one for guests. And don't forget an umbrella and raincoat. It may be July, but pack for October. We'll be lucky if the thermometer hits seventy."

"Yes, honey. And don't you mean twenty-one?"

"Huh?"

"Celsius. Seventy degrees is twenty-one Celsius. You're on Celsius, right?"

"Wow! Impressive. I've been here three years and still haven't converted."

"Don't get too excited. Dolores may be a know-it-all, but she's useful. Gave me a cheat sheet. Conversions for temperatures and money as well as a handful of French phrases—*oui, merci beau*-cup, bone-jure, *comment* tolley-*vouz*."

Grinning, Jack nodded at the camera. "What, no Flemish?"

June gasped. "You're right. She didn't give me any. Guess I could try to get by with French. You know, 'A' for effort and all that."

"Oh no, don't do that. The Flemish speak wonderful English. As a matter of fact, they prefer it to French. There's a fairly large language divide over here. A real sore spot."

"You don't say. Well there's a scoop I got for Dolores."

In their many conversations leading up to the trip, Jack tried to prepare June for Brussels. He didn't want to pull off her rose-colored glasses, but he didn't want her to be disappointed either. He knew his mother had an idealized vision of Europe garnered chiefly from romantic movies of the fifties and sixties. The old boy-meets-girl, boy-loses-girl, boy-gets-girl routine set amid ruins, luxury hotels, brilliant landscapes, and a lush, symphonic soundtrack. Europe, in his mother's mind, was a sophisticated land of fashionable cafés, magnificent squares, tree-lined boulevards, and lots of chic, witty white people.

Jack loved his adopted home. He chose to look past its many imperfections. Why spoil an amazing adventure? The food was great but service lackluster. And with the exception of the Grand Place, Jack assumed Brussels wouldn't live up to his mother's ideal. Sure, the city had its charms, including some very beautiful and historic places. But the Brussels in which Jack lived was rather grimy, run down, and tired.

For Jack, however, Brussels represented more than a physical place—much more. Putting an ocean between himself and Milwaukee liberated him in a way that he had never imagined. He was free to be the real Jack Ramsey for the first time in his life. For that reason alone, he had great fondness for Brussels. Perhaps he always would.

Jack drove his company Audi to Zaventem, parked in the short-term lot, and headed to the arrivals area. He wanted June to see a familiar face the moment she cleared customs. He had a colleague, a fellow American expat, to thank for the cellophane-wrapped bouquet he carried in his hand.

"Can't meet your mom at the airport without flowers," Tony had said. "She wouldn't say anything if you came empty-handed, but believe me, buddy boy, the inspection will go better if you do."

"Inspection?"

"Jacky boy, this is no ordinary visitor. This is your *mother*. It's an inspection, tougher than any I ever faced in the army reserve. Put a vase of flowers in her room. Every morning when she wakes up, and every night before she goes to bed, the sight and smell of them will remind her what a good son you are. She'll go easy on you, overlook the dirty bathroom, stained rug, shabby neighborhood, et cetera. Don't get me wrong, there'll be judgmental sneers and raised eyebrows. Can't get away from those. But the sweet smell of roses will temper their severity."

Jack laughed. His mother wasn't like that, not really. She had her likes, dislikes, and opinions, but she wasn't overbearing as many of his friends' mothers. When his father was alive, the family home simply wasn't large enough for two big personalities. June, bowing to her husband's need to command center stage, seldom ventured into the spotlight. Jack considered her more than merely his parent. June was his friend. Nonetheless, Tony's advice was sound. Flowers couldn't hurt—a bit of insurance for a modest sum.

Jack stood on the airport's lower level, elbow-to-elbow with others waiting for loved ones. Some readied themselves to snap photos of the reunions. Looking around, Jack wondered whether he should have created a sign with his mother's name. June would have gotten a kick out of that. Jack fished his phone out of his pocket and readied the camera app. He'd post his mother's joy-filled face on Facebook for his brother and her Starbucks ladies.

With a bouquet in one hand, Jack lifted his phone to line up the shot. As he took a few practice photos, he felt a tap on his shoulder. The tap became harder, almost a shove. When Jack turned, a dark-haired, bearded man rattled off something in French.

"English?" Jack asked. "Do you speak English?"

The question infuriated the man. Again he rattled something off in French, adding, "No photo, no photo," as he gestured toward a frail-looking man, white-haired and bearded. The old guy wore a cream-colored tunic. His intense dark-eyed stare made Jack uneasy.

"No photo, no photo," the shoulder tapper repeated. Two more men sidled up to the old guy. After a brief exchange among themselves, they also glared at Jack.

Jack nodded. "I understand. *Je comprends*. No photo, no photo."

The man moved his hand toward Jack's phone. "Delete, or I call police."

Jack was flustered. He felt his heart race. He didn't want any trouble. Some cultures, he knew, considered photos a theft of a person's soul. Whatever the issue, it didn't matter. Jack was outnumbered. He fumbled with the camera app. "I delete, I delete," he stammered, sending the photos to the digital trash bin. He held up the phone. "All gone." The man offered one final glare before returning to his group.

As Jack sought a new waiting spot, he thought of his mother. He didn't want her rose-colored glasses to fall off so quickly. He weaved through the crowd, sizing up other bystanders before settling next to a column near a coffee shop. Passengers started to emerge through the sliding opaque doors of customs, first a trickle, then a steady flow. Only when a husky fellow bent down to pick up a fallen Chicago Cubs baseball cap did Jack see June. At the sight of his petite mother, a sense of delight overwhelmed him. His eyes moistened with tears.

A shock of white hair was his mother's most prominent feature, followed by her clear kind eyes and pink round face. Under an open raincoat, she wore a green sweater and on her feet, bright white sneakers. She let go of the handle of a large spinner suitcase to say goodbye to a fellow passenger, treating the young blonde as if they were old friends. Jack cringed as he conjured up an image of his mother asking for the woman's contact information to share with her "handsome and very successful son."

"Mom, Mom," Jack yelled. "Over here."

June's face lit up. When Jack raised his camera-readied phone, June struck a series of movie-star poses before waving him off with her hand.

There were tears in her eyes when she threw her arms out for a hug. She held on as if she'd never let go. "Sorry, honey," she said through sniffles. "Don't mean to be a blubbering idiot."

"It's okay, it's okay." Jack kissed her cheek, catching a whiff of the floral perfume that she reserved for special occasions. The scent brought back vivid images of family weddings and funerals. Jack pulled a tissue from his jeans pocket. "Here, wipe your eyes."

"I came prepared," she replied, pulling a pack of travel tissues from her coat. After Jack presented her with the roses, she teared up again. "I…I'm so happy to see you, honey."

After blowing her nose, she drew her arm out of the coat sleeve. "Here, honey, help me off with this. I'm burning up. The way you talked, I expected Alaska." Her expression turned serious as she scanned the arrivals area.

"What are you looking for?"

"Muslims," she whispered. "Your Uncle Jim warned me. Says Belgium's 'infected with 'em.'"

Jack recoiled at the absurdity. His mother's older brother was a cable news junkie, as conservative and intolerant as Jack's late father. His uncle and father were high school buddies and football jocks who worked together at the brewery until his father's death. A fan of border walls, Uncle Jim frequently bellowed at the TV and wrote rambling letters to the editor complaining about activist judges' violating God's will. Jack hoped his mother was more open-minded although he wasn't certain. She seldom contradicted her husband's emphatic opinions. Still, Jack was glad June hadn't witnessed the incident with his camera. As for himself, he had a few Muslim work buddies. He loved tagine dinners and had even dated a Turk.

IN BRUGES…AGAIN

"You didn't want to go to Bruges; now you want to spend a couple of nights." June sat at Jack's small kitchen table and studied her son over a coffee cup. Though in Brussels for only three days, she'd established a morning routine—croissants from a local boulangerie smothered with rich European butter and strawberry jam and Starbucks coffee.

Jack turned, inserting a bowl of instant oatmeal into the microwave. "Lots to see in Bruges. We don't want to rush things." He studied his mother in the glass reflection.

She shook her head, clearly unconvinced. "Okay, if that's what you want."

"We can explore Ghent, all of Flanders, really. Then there's the coast and…Antwerp, yes, Antwerp. Can't miss Antwerp. Maybe stay a night or two there, as well."

"You said we could see all these places as day trips. Seems silly to waste money on hotels when you have this beautiful new apartment."

"Nothing's silly for my mother's first trip to Europe. It'll be exciting for me to see Bruges at night. Never done that before."

Where his rationale came from, Jack didn't know. But he was proud of his brilliance. June stopped arguing. He made the overnight visits appear as if she were doing him a favor. What mother couldn't resist? Little did June know that Jack had an urgent and secret reason to get her out of his apartment for a few days.

The prior afternoon, while a jetlagged June napped, Jack had sat in his living room, surfing the Internet and listening to classical music. A commotion outside the front door got his attention, then he heard rattling. *A key in the lock.* He sprang up from the sofa, reaching the front hall just as the door opened.

He gasped. Before him stood Karl. Thick dark hair crowned his six-foot-two frame. A black T-shirt accentuated a muscular chest and thick biceps. Jeans tightened around his bulging thighs and calves.

Jack stammered. "Wh…what are you doing here?"

"Nice to see you too, Johnny boy," the handsome German replied. "I live here, remember?"

"Used to. B…but you don't anymore. We've been through that," Jack said, looking over his shoulder to the closed door of the guest room. "You gotta leave."

Jack and Karl had dated for more than a year. Six months into their relationship, Karl gave up his apartment and moved in with Jack. For a time, Jack thought the German expat might be *the* guy. But two months before, the couple hit a rocky patch. Bickering grew more frequent, ending in a shouting match. Jack didn't recall whether he threw Karl out or Karl left of his own accord.

At the time, Jack convinced himself that the breakup was all for the best. But recently, he'd begun to analyze it. Did his mother's impending visit have something to do with the split? Did a subconscious compulsion to guard his secret drive him to sabotage the relationship? After all, Karl wasn't a bad person. On the contrary, the Berlin lawyer was kind, intelligent, and nurturing, if just a bit stubborn.

Jack blocked the entryway, his stance wide. "You moved out."

"Oh, that," said Karl with a wink. "Only temporary. I drove home. Joined my parents for a summer holiday." Carrying two suitcases, Karl moved deeper into the apartment, pushing past Jack.

"But us. Er…um, I mean there is no *us* anymore."

Karl shrugged. "*Ja, ja, ja.* I understand. Maybe we can talk about that?"

Jack folded his arms across his chest. "No, *nein*. We're done, finished, kaput."

"I can sleep in the guest room if you like."

Jack gasped. "No! My mother's in there."

A look of surprise swept over Karl's face. "Your mother. I forgot about her visit. I can sleep on the couch." He peered into the living room.

"No! You have to leave."

"I've nowhere to go."

"There must be a friend, a hotel, some place."

"You're tossing me out?"

"Yes."

Karl dropped his suitcases. "Then I stay. As much my apartment as it is yours."

"Nonsense."

"Paid half the rent, remember? You used it to buy that fancy TV." Karl nodded toward the giant flat-screen television mounted above the fireplace.

Jack cringed. Karl was right. He had paid Jack three months' rent in advance. Since Jack's employer covered his housing, he used Karl's share of the rent to buy some luxuries like the TV and a new computer.

Jack moved to the desk and picked up his wallet. "Here, I'll pay you back, or pay for a hotel. But you can't stay here."

"Contract's a contract. I stay."

Jack knew he couldn't win that legal battle. He spent the next thirty minutes pleading with Karl in whispers, fearful that his mother would awaken and discover them. Finally, they agreed on a plan. Karl would leave for one night, returning the next evening. Jack would spirit June out of town. The end of the month, the expiration of Karl's binding contract, was less than a week away. By the time Jack and his mother returned to Brussels, Karl would be gone from Jack's life once and for all, legally if not emotionally.

———

Jack decided to drive to Bruges. A car gave them more flexibility and made for a quicker getaway. He still worried that Karl might pop by just to stir the pot. Their last argument, the one that led to the breakup, had concerned Karl's frustration with Jack's refusal to tell his family about his lover. Jack had stammered, unable to come up with a good answer why he wouldn't tell his mother about the man he supposedly loved.

June settled into the Audi and fastened her seat belt. "You know what today is?"

Jack shook his head as he pulled away from the curb. "The twenty-sixth?"

"No, Tuesday. If it's Tuesday, this must be Belgium," she said with a hearty laugh. "You remember, the movie. Suzanne Pleshette, Ian something or other, and oodles of cameos. Been dying to use that. Drove my Starbucks ladies crazy with that line for weeks. Dolores just rolled her eyes."

Jack chuckled. "You and your movies. Speaking of which, did you watch *In Bruges*?"

June groaned. "Got it from the library after you mentioned it. Weird. Thick Irish accents. Had to call your brother to figure out how to turn on the subtitles. Better without. Oh, the foul language. Even worse than your father's."

"Sorry." He'd forgotten about the movie's profanity. He loved the humor, not to mention Colin Farrell's rugged good looks. Jack often advised houseguests to watch the dark comedy before a visit, to better appreciate Bruges.

June tapped his leg. "Oh, honey, don't be sorry. You know I don't go in for violent pictures. Bruges looked fabulous. Even in winter. Star of the movie if you ask me."

After checking into their hotel, Jack and his mother explored the city. He took her first to the Grote Markt, where they shared *pommes frites* in the shadow of the twelfth-century Belfry. Although she was an avid walker, June decided to pass on the 366 stairs to the top. With mayonnaise clinging to a *frite* in her hand, she gazed up the facade of the red-brick tower to the large clock. "Wouldn't want to climb all the way up just to fall off."

"That was only in the movie, Mom. And the guy didn't fall, he jumped—to warn his buddy."

"He shoulda texted."

IN BRUGES...AGAIN

Jack put his arm around his mother and laughed. After a stop at his favorite chocolate shop where they sampled bacon- and vodka-flavored bonbons, Jack guided June to the five-hundred-year-old Church of Our Lady. The Gothic structure housed a Michelangelo, the only one of the artist's sculptures to leave Italy in his lifetime. In the three years that Jack had been bringing out-of-town visitors, he'd never seen the church's interior without scaffolding. The scent of sawdust mingled with those of stale incense and candle wax.

"Oh! Oh!" June exclaimed upon entering the side altar that housed the statue. "This was in that George Clooney picture, *Monuments Men* I think. Not my favorite movie, but with George Clooney, who the hell cares. It was at the end. Decades later. His real-life father brings his grandson—hmm, wonder if the kid was his real grandson. Anyway," she added with a shrug, "George's father brings the kid here to show him the statue he saved from the Nazis. Wait till I tell my Starbucks ladies. Dolores will flip. Better yet, get a photo of me with the Madonna. It'll impress the girls *and* Father Dougherty."

After the photo, June emptied her change purse to light a dozen offertory candles including one for each of her boys. June wore her faith on her chest, literally. Her aunt and godmother was a pious nun. She had gifted her goddaughter a silver cross blessed by some pope. June was never without it. When Jack was an infant, June, in one of her rare displays of authority, made her husband drive the family to Chicago to see the Polish pope. She insisted upon her sons going to confession and volunteered them up as altar boys despite their griping about the early morning wakeups.

Between his father's rigid beliefs and his mother's faith, discussion of Jack's sexuality was out of the question. Unlike his father, Jack's mother never denounced homosexuality, but with a Bible prominently displayed on the family's coffee table, and crucifixes nailed above every bed as well as the kitchen table, she didn't have to.

After June lit candles and prayed in a pew, Jack suggested lunch. He usually took visitors to the same place, a nice restaurant opposite the church. For Bruges, it wasn't too touristy and the food was good. A large veranda protected by a yellow awning was perfect for people-watching. Jack ordered salmon. His mother, at his suggestion, had the *moules-frites*. They both drank Chardonnay.

June glanced across the courtyard. "Lovely, just lovely. You're so lucky to have so many beautiful old churches. Ours back home look like supermarkets."

"You still going to mass, Mom?"

She lifted her chin. "Every Sunday. Started attending weekday services too."

Jack was torn. He was happy that church provided his mother meaning, a refuge from loneliness. But he was concerned that her growing dependence on religion might drive a wedge between them when he finally told her the truth about his sexuality.

June must have sensed his consternation. "I know what you're thinking, honey. I'm not going to leave the church all my money."

"B…but, that's not—"

"Figure of speech, Jackaroo. I know you don't care about my money. My church-going is as much social as spiritual. I'm not becoming one of those holy-roller types like my mother. They're nice people. Most of 'em anyway." She leaned across the table and lowered her voice. "Before you say it, I want you to know…that I…that I know.…"

His breathing stalled. *What does she know?* He tried to appear calm. He put down his wineglass, afraid that his quivering fingers would betray his anxiety.

"I know you don't go to church. Your brother doesn't either. It used to make me sad. But your life is your life."

Throughout lunch, his mother's words kept ringing in his head: *your life is your life*. Did she really mean that—about *all* things?

They skipped dessert and walked around the corner to the canal. Jack considered the boat tours the best attraction in Bruges. Brimming with tourists, flat-bottom boats glided under the town's charming stone bridges. On the tour, June sat in awe, her eyes glued to the centuries-old buildings along the banks. She turned to Jack, a look of joy on her face. "Best trip ever, kiddo. Thanks for bringing me to Bruges."

Her ears perked at the mention of Fidel, a local celebrity seen in the first ten minutes of *In Bruges*. "There he is," she shouted to Jack. "Get a picture, get a picture." She grinned as she posed below the gabled window in which the handsome golden lab lounged. "Fidel's the only one in the picture without a foul mouth," she said, drawing laughter from some of the other tourists in the boat. After sitting back down, June leaned her head back and laughed to the sky like a little girl. Jack was thrilled. The holiday had brought them closer together. Why would he want to say or do anything to spoil that?

After pressing Jack to give the boat's driver a good tip, June asked to go back to the hotel. She was tired and wanted a nap before dinner. "Maybe that adorable man will still be at the front desk."

"Franco?" Jack tried not to sound too interested. But he knew exactly who his mother meant. Tall, dark, and handsome, Franco had checked them into their rooms earlier that morning. He was gorgeous in an Armani suit and red silk tie. A warm and friendly personality made him even more attractive. His sexy accent was a bonus. Jack didn't know if Franco was gay. European men were hard to read.

"*Oui, oui, certainement,* Franco." She gasped as her hand flew to her mouth. "Oh my, *French.*" Her eyes darted from side to side.

Jack hugged her. "It's okay, Mom. No Flemish patrols in the area. Didn't you notice the boatman spoke English, German, Flemish, *and* French?"

She bobbed her head. "I'm so impressed at all the languages everyone speaks over here. I know folks back home who can barely speak English. Look at Franco." Jack hadn't stopped looking at Franco—in reality, more ogling than looking. "He speaks English, Italian, German, Dutch, and Spanish. And those were just the ones I caught while we waited in line. No ring either."

"Mom!" Jack understood his mother's meaning. He had scanned Franco's fingers as well.

"Don't Mom me. He's quite the catch."

Jack merely offered a pursed-lip smile.

As they walked back to the hotel and his mother raved about Bruges, Jack's mind wandered elsewhere. He knew he had to tell her. Karl was right. It had been unfair of Jack to keep their relationship a secret, unfair to everyone—Karl, June, and himself. He decided that he had to tell his mother before she left Belgium. He might remain overseas for years. And if he did repatriate, it probably wouldn't be to Milwaukee. As for Karl, too many nasty things had been said to salvage that relationship. There would be other Karls, he hoped. He didn't want to mess up again.

When Jack and his mother entered the hotel, Franco offered a warm smile from behind the reception desk. "Good evening, Ramseys. Trust you had an enjoyable day touring Bruges."

June approached the desk. "Bruges is fabulous," she gushed. "My handsome son Jack here could be an official tour guide," she added, pulling an embarrassed Jack to her side. "He knows everything about the city." She listed the sites they visited, boasting again of Jack's knowledge.

Jack felt his face warm. "Thanks, Mom. I'm sure Franco is pretty busy. Let's ask for a recommendation for dinner and get out of his way."

Franco shook his head. "No bother at all. I enjoy talking to our guests." His dark eyes focused on Jack. "With all your knowledge, you must be aware, then, of the historical treasure located right here in our hotel?"

"Bet he knows all about it. Don't you, honey?" Motherly pride filled June's tone.

With both sets of eyes on him, Jack swallowed hard. "Actually, I don't."

Franco explained that excavation crews building the hotel had uncovered ancient foundations. They discovered a ninth-century fort used for defense against Vikings. Later, a large church occupied the site, surviving until Napoleon ordered it demolished in 1799. Afraid of preservationists halting construction, the hotel's owners granted public access to the ruins as long as the lower-level conference rooms were not in use.

"Lots of interesting relics down there," Franco said. "I can give you a tour if you like."

June turned to Jack. "We'd love a tour, right?"

After arranging for a backup, Franco led Jack and his mother down the staircase to the ruins. The walls were magnificent. One area contained well-preserved sections of the church's choir gallery. Franco was kind, funny, and intelligent. His grasp of Belgian history including Bruges impressed mother and son. If June weren't there, Jack might have been tempted to flirt with their guide.

During the tour, Jack's phone beeped. It was a text from Karl, something about a water leak in the flat. Jack excused himself to call from the lobby. When he returned, June was alone, sitting at a conference table, sipping wine. Two waffles and a fresh beer were set on the table.

June gestured Jack to sit. She nodded toward the items on the table. "Franco's treat. He's such a sweet man."

"He shouldn't have done that. Probably comes out of his own pocket. Hotels aren't known for good pay and generosity."

"He can afford it. *Well* he can," she added responding to Jack's scowl. "Franco owns the hotel."

Jack looked at her as if she were crazy. "What?"

"Franco owns the hotel. Or rather, his family does. Others across Europe too. I'm guessing he's a millionaire. Just like in the movies."

June explained how she found a hotel brochure in the conference room. On the back was a picture of the owners, a beautiful Italian family. She spotted Franco immediately, dimpled chin and all. Embarrassed by June's discovery, Franco said that he preferred to keep his position a secret. His father wanted his children to learn the business from the ground up.

"He's gay."

Jack sprayed a mouthful of beer. "What?"

"Franco's gay." She slid the brochure in front of Jack, her fingers on the family photo. "His two brothers have wives. So I asked him where Mrs. Franco was."

"You didn't?"

"I'm getting bolder in my old age," she said with a mischievous grin. "Anyway, that's when Franco told me. He's gay. Single too."

Jack scrutinized his mother's face. There was no judgmental sneer or raised eyebrow. Maybe the confrontation with Karl primed him, or perhaps Bruges had cast its magic spell with the aid of a handsome Italian millionaire. Jack seized the moment.

"Mom, there's something I need to tell you."

Smiling, she reached across the table and squeezed his arm. "You're gay."

"H…how did you know?"

"Oh, honey, I've had my suspicions since you turned down taking Sally Simmons to the prom. Sweetest girl in school, and pretty as a peach. I never knew for certain. Figured I'd wait for you to tell me." Looking at Jack with kindness in her eyes, she took his hand. "I'm glad there are no more secrets."

"So you're okay with…with my being gay?"

June leaned over and kissed Jack's cheek. "Honey, your life is your life. I made the mistake of listening to my mother."

"Grandma?"

June nodded. "Shortly after I got married, she told me to never forget the *obey* part of my wedding vow. 'Recipe for a happy marriage,' she said." June heaved a sigh. Her meaning was clear.

"I'm sorry Mom."

June managed a smile. "Don't be. I got two handsome boys out of the deal. But learn from my mistake. Live your own life. Remember, you're my baby, Johnny. I'll always love you, no matter what."

"And your church?"

"Doesn't trump family. Hateful people don't belong in church anyway," June said, reaching for a waffle.

They sat in silence out of respect for the special moment they shared. Jack was overwhelmed with a sense of relief. He felt serenity, peace, freedom, and deep love for his mother.

June's sudden and deep laugh echoed off the ancient stone walls. Jack turned. Powdered sugar sprinkled like confetti from his mother's face.

"What's come over you?"

"Thank you, honey, thank you. I got Dolores beat hands down. She never stops bragging about her gay nephew. Wait till she hears that I got a gay son." Impish delight returned to her eyes. "Now go and ask out that adorable Franco before someone else does. That is, if you see yourself coming back to Bruges."

Jack grinned. "Are you kidding? Bruges is amazing. I can see myself in Bruges again and again."

Will-o'-the-Wisp

"Getting too old," Edward muttered as he shaded his eyes. Light streamed through sheer curtains onto his platform bed. Despite a growing intensity of hangover-related symptoms, the self-proclaimed party animal had no plans to curb his alcohol intake.

He slid his hand down the satin sheet. He wasn't surprised that she was gone. Sweet, innocent Emily wasn't the happiest of conquests. No sooner had her orgasmic sighs subsided than she mumbled regrets at her deflowering. *Poor thing, probably sitting through every morning mass till she rubs the luster from her rosary beads.* Edward sent a stifled laugh to the plaster ceiling. He figured that once pious Emily went to confession—wiped her slate clean, so to speak—the little minx would be back for more.

He considered those like Emily who sought comfort in scripture and ceremony, to be fools, weaklings, or worse, hypocrites. Sex was Edward's religion. His was a deep faith rooted in the tenets of self-interest, instant gratification, control, and carnal pleasure. As for the people who dreamed up the notion of heaven, confession, and all the other silly superstitious mumbo jumbo, Edward called them *brilliant manipulators*, scaremongers who recognized that hope and salvation were as marketable as life insurance and fitness club memberships.

Although disdainful of organized religion, Edward Crane, nonetheless, profited handsomely from it. He relished the irony. As a staunch atheist, he earned a good living as the Vice President of Sales for Europe's largest distributor of religious trinkets and paraphernalia. He never considered the ethical dilemma of selling wares to the very churches and religious institutions he scorned. On the contrary, his company's near-monopoly pricing of cheap goods made in China filled him with great satisfaction—his very own ticket to paradise.

With his head pounding, Edward rolled onto his side and pushed the bedcovers from his naked body. He padded across the planked floor to the white porcelain bathroom. His reflection squinted back at him in the mirror—eyes bloodshot and puffy, his ruddy face days overdue for a shave. Blinking away the haggard image, Edward opened the medicine cabinet. Aspirin tablets resisted his attempts to pop them from their plastic casings. He chewed them out of their packaging and spit the foil covers into the sink. After downing the pills, he splashed water on his face, peed, and returned to the bedroom.

He grabbed his phone from the nightstand and plopped backward onto the bed. He'd lost count of the tolling chimes from a nearby church, but the phone screen informed him that it was eleven o'clock. His headache-induced frown turned into a smirk at the sight of Lucie's text.

Knew she'd come back; they always do. Still, twelve weeks of silence pushed the limits on lover's remorse, *his* lovers anyway. Then again, Lucie was as innocent and as naïve as a lamb. That's how he liked them, choosing his conquests from the flock of inexperienced women defenseless against a little attention and flattery. Lucie was an ideal target. Managing the small, cluttered gift shop inside Brussels' cathedral, she spent her days surrounded by saints, her mind steeped in superstition.

He tapped the phone for Lucie's full message. "W, I overreacted. Huge mistake. Love to see you again…if you'll have me. L."

Edward's confidence surged. *Even a holy roller*, he thought, *worries about such mundane matters as rent and utilities*. His dangled carrot of a high-paying job with his company was usually his most successful pitch before, during, and after the seduction. His mind churned with images of Lucie, mental snapshots of the first and only time they had sex. He'd pursued the virgin princess for weeks, wasting many an evening priming her with pricey wine, posh menus, and small talk. His breakthrough came with the expensive weekend getaway. He grinned at his bedroom ceiling, picturing Lucie's naked surrender in the ancient inn. The quivering maiden reclined on the four-poster bed, preparing to reward her hero and savior with her virtue.

The events that finally landed Lucie's acquiescence were indeed serendipitous. Edward had never been so grateful for a foolish legend to "seal the deal," setting the stage for his fiendishly clever seduction. Perhaps he was being too modest. Fate may have led the couple to Diepenbeek, a small Limburg village near the Dutch border, but he was the one who recognized the opportunity and seized it with both hands and a thrusting pelvis. Awaiting the aspirin's soothing powers, Edward closed his eyes recalling the triumphant weekend three months in the past when, at last, he lured the reluctant Lucie into his bed.

As Lucie readied herself upstairs in her room for dinner, Edward waited with anticipation in the public room of the Duke of Brabant Inn. He'd told her to make herself over-the-top gorgeous. He booked a table in a Michelin-starred restaurant. He didn't argue when she insisted on separate accommodations. It wasn't so much about how a weekend started or even how it ended. What mattered most was what happened in between. He was optimistic he'd get Lucie into his bed. *But how?* That question occupied his thoughts as he threw back a glass of rich, nutty Belgian beer.

Most of the chattering around him at the bar was in Flemish, a language undecipherable to his English ears. After two years living and working in Brussels, Edward managed only basic French, enough to order a meal and flirt with pretty women. "*Voulez-vous coucher avec moi, ce soir?"* wasn't offered as proof of his musical prowess but as a bona fide proposition.

As Edward placed his glass onto the marble tabletop, two middle-aged couples entered the room. Behind them swaggered a fair-haired young man, tall, husky, and broad-shouldered. Sea-blue eyes with a square jaw, cleft chin, and infectious smile made him handsome. The newcomers spoke English, the couples with a flat North American accent. The young man's clipped speech with exaggerated hard consonants and elongated vowels marked him as Flemish. He was the only one of the party not toting a suitcase.

The innkeeper, a burly and affable fellow who doubled as the barman, grinned. Clasping the younger man's shoulder, he extended a greeting in Flemish. The younger man, whose name Edward picked up as Hugo, responded in English, "Guiding these nice people through the Flemish countryside before we hit Brussels. Dr. Chamberlain's a colleague, so to speak, a fellow professor. She teaches European Civ at the University of Toronto." Hugo nodded to a tall, slim woman. She fit Edward's stereotype of a drab, uninteresting academic: no makeup, jeans and denim jacket, sensible shoes, long hair streaked with gray, and thick dark-rimmed glasses. "The professor brought along the mister as well as her brother and his wife, the Pratchers," Hugo added. The North Americans smiled, bobbing their heads in unison. "They signed up for my Church and Folklore tour."

The barkeeper nodded to the Canadians. "You folks sure picked the right guy. Hugo knows every nook, corner, and legend of Limburg. Bet he'll even stir up a few of our local ghosts for your pleasure." The innkeeper turned toward Hugo, cocking his head. "But I've only got the two rooms for your clients. Full up otherwise."

Could volunteer to give up my room and bunk in with Lucie, Edward thought to himself with a quiet chuckle.

"Gonna spend the night at the farm with Mom," Hugo replied, dashing Edward's plans. "Don't trek over here from Maastricht often enough to suit her."

"I know your mother," the innkeeper replied with a few nods of his head. "She's never forgiven her baby boy for choosing the university over his prized horses, cows, and mother."

Hugo laughed, more pride than embarrassment in his manner. "I'll gain five kilos before my visit's done, that's for sure. I'm guessing she's been baking for a week."

Even with that brief introduction, Edward thought his own mother a stark contrast to the young guide's. Ursula as Edward called her, never Mother or Mom, was only too happy to pack her "baby boy" off to boarding school. Prayed the good fathers might succeed where her Bible verses and leather strap failed—to banish the devil within him. Eight-year-old Edward was doubly happy to escape his mother's unforgiving fanaticism. Having wished Ursula dead for so many years, it no longer mattered whether the Cornish churchyard in her village had finally claimed her sanctimonious corpse. She was dead to him.

After a round of introductions, the touring party accepted the innkeeper's offer of a welcome drink. They settled down at two tables beside Edward, apologizing for crowding him with their luggage. The congenial innkeeper extended the same courtesy to Edward, who downed the remainder of his beer before handing over his glass for the free refill.

The professor's husband, Fred, raised his glass for a communal toast. "Bring it on all ye ghosts and goblins, and all the other creatures of the night. We're ready for you."

Ann Pratcher, a small, mousy woman flinched. "Oh my. Please don't provoke the spirits, Fred."

Her husband, Donald, the professor's overweight brother, put his arm around his wife's shoulder. "Don't you fret, honeybee. Your big, brave guy will protect you. That is, unless one of those spirits is an adorable blonde with big titties. In that case, you're on your own."

A man after my own heart, thought Edward with a silent snicker.

While her husband merely rolled his eyes, Dr. Chamberlain shot her brother a stinging scowl before addressing the entire group. "There are no such things as ghosts. Tell them, Hugo. Merely foolish legends easily explained by natural phenomena, overactive imaginations, tourist boards, and alcohol."

Pulling a face, Edward stared into his beer. *What a prude! Too smart for her own good.*

Hugo shrugged. "Don't know, Dr. Chamberlain. We have a bit more history with ghosts this side of the Atlantic—"

The innkeeper interrupted. "You brought 'em here for the Schoverik, didn't you, Hugo?"

Hugo replied with a broad grin that dimpled his cheeks. "I was saving that surprise for later. But nothing like liquor to grease the gab."

The two couples stared at him, their expressions ranging from interest and amusement to fear and doubt. Curious himself, Edward returned his smart phone to his pocket. Even the innkeeper, after refilling everyone's glass, poured himself a beer and sat down to listen.

Hugo took a large gulp of dark ale before beginning his yarn. "Folks who live in these parts are known as the Schoverik. Before I tell you why, make me one promise." He waited until his clients nodded their assent. "Don't whistle till we're safely out of town. Could be a matter of life—or death." For the next twenty minutes the handsome young man enthralled his audience with a macabre tale of the supernatural.

That evening, Lucie sat in the passenger seat of Edward's black BMW. She eyed him warily as he undid his seat belt, concern on her face. "Thought you didn't like walks."

"True, messes with Italian shoe leather. But the good people back at the inn said this stroll isn't to be missed. Besides, I can use a little exercise after that seven-course meal," Edward added with a pat to his stomach.

Lucie gazed out the car's side window. "You sure about this?"

Edward stared at Lucie's reflection. Her perfect, pale face stood out against the backdrop of a pitch-black forest. Observing the fragile innocence in her eyes, he felt his heart race. Excitement surged throughout his body.

Following the innkeeper's directions, Edward had pulled the car off the main road, driving several hundred yards down a gravel path before coming to a dead-end. They appeared to be in the middle of a primeval forest. A full moon, the same one that lent an air of romance to the restaurant terrace, disappeared behind clusters of clouds in the plum-colored sky. The fickle moon soon returned, casting an eerie glow through blankets of fog that settled into ravines and dells such as the one in which the couple found themselves.

"Come on, honeybee. Your big, brave guy will protect you." Lucie's release of her shoulder harness thwarted Edward's attempt to kiss her cheek.

Edward led Lucie through a densely wooded path, the air laden with the fresh, earthy scents of midsummer. After walking several yards over the moist ground, Edward stopped. "Don't suppose we'll run into the Schoverik, do you?"

"The what?"

"The Schoverik. Back in England, we call them will-o'-the-wisp."

"Never heard of it."

"Not it, *them*." Edward was pleased with the look of fear that flashed in Lucie's eyes. "Come on, sweetie," he added, grabbing her hand and pulling her forward toward what looked to be the clearing mentioned by the innkeeper. "Nothing to worry about—I hope. But best not to whistle, just in case."

"Not to whistle? Why not?"

He assumed a somber expression. "Best not to, that's all. Merely a precaution."

"If you're trying to scare me, you're doing a good job."

He lifted her hand to his lips and kissed it. "Let's climb the embankment. Fog's not so thick up there. Want to show you something. Folks at the inn said there's a lovely pond—perfect for a romantic walk."

Over Lucie's objections of climbing the hill in a narrow skirt and high heels, Edward coaxed her along, guiding her up the steep incline. As he held her close, a whiff of jasmine perfume, one of his early gifts intended to prime her submission, nearly intoxicated him.

When they reached the top of the ridge, Lucie gasped. "That's no pond; it's a swamp."

"I prefer marsh," Edward replied, gazing across the expansive wetlands dotted with puffs of fog.

Hugo and the innkeeper hadn't exaggerated when they called the area a godforsaken cesspool. In the fleeting moments when the moon broke through the cloud cover, the scene was even bleaker. Petrified limbs of half-submerged trees reached skyward resembling bony fingers clawing their way out of a watery grave. Putrid odors of rotting plants rose from green, stale water. Marsh grasses swayed as if blown by the foul breath of the devil himself.

Perfect, Edward thought, *simply perfect*.

Lucie sidled up closer to him. "This place is ghastly. Let's get out of here."

"I swear I didn't know. I'll have a talk with the innkeeper." Still, Edward didn't budge. He scanned the horizon, squinting from one direction to the other. *They simply must be here*.

Lucie's grip tightened. "Wh…what's that?"

Detecting fear in Lucie's voice, Edward followed her gaze and gasped. The scene was even more ghoulish than Hugo's extraordinary narrative suggested. At the swamp's edge where giant willows bent their branches toward the murky water, lights flickered above the reeds and cattails—balls of fire the size of men's heads. Some moved; others remained perfectly still. Each glowed, flashed, sparked.

"Schoverik," Edward whispered, surprised by the apprehension in his own voice. If his scheme were to work, he'd have to get hold of himself.

Lucie grabbed him even tighter, her fingers pressed into his arm. "What are they?" As she buried her face into his chest, the smell of strawberry wafted from her hair, stirring his passion, reaffirming his mission.

"No one knows for sure. Some say marsh gas. Decomposing matter. Might explain why they form over swamps—and graveyards."

Lucie shuddered. "Dead bodies."

"Sure. Rotting corpses, dead trees, and other organic matter."

"But nothing supernatural? Nothing to be afraid of?"

Edward sensed that Lucie was trying to talk herself out of a full-blown panic attack. He didn't want her to succeed—not yet. He gazed down at the top of her head, a mischievous smirk turning up the corners of his mouth. "Others claim the will-o'-the-wisps are spirits. Eternal wanderers. Souls trapped between life and death, toying with any hapless fool who stumbles upon them."

"But are they evil? Do they aim to harm?"

"No one knows. It's said if a person dares to approach, the lights float away, always beyond reach. If you retreat, they pursue." Feeling Lucie shudder in his arms, he added, "Guess we could test that theory." He took a step forward toward the hovering fireballs.

Pulling him back to her side, Lucie stammered, "P…please, Edward. L…let's go."

He wrapped his arms around her. She surrendered as he drew her into a firm embrace. "No Schoverik's going to catch you, precious girl. I won't let them."

As they turned to begin the descent from the steep embankment, Edward pretended to twist his ankle. He dropped to the grass and groaned, clutching his foot in dramatic fashion.

Lucie shrieked. "You okay?"

"Close call," he replied before releasing a whistle. "Could have broken my neck."

Lucie's eyes widened; her mouth fell open.

"What's wrong?" he asked, affecting concern.

"You…you whistled."

"What?"

"Edward, you whistled. You warned me not to whistle."

Feigning surprise, he gasped; his hand flew to his open mouth. "I…I didn't mean to." He looked over his shoulder toward the swamp for effect. "We…we should be okay," he added. "Help me to the car, quick." He laced his tone with urgency and concern as he lifted himself off the grass and hobbled on one leg.

"Why did you warn me not to whistle?"

"It's nothing—nothing."

Lucie grabbed his arm. "You just don't want me to panic. Tell me, Edward, tell me." Her nails dug deeper through the fabric of his jacket.

Edward was enjoying his little game. He heaved an exaggerated sigh. "Legend has it that if you whistle in the presence of a Schoverik, it'll pursue you. One poor soul from Diepenbeek, the story goes, made the mistake of whistling at the ghoulish lights."

"What happened?"

"Schoverik took chase. The man ran for his life. Made his way home, slammed his door shut, and bolted it against the spirit. Safe inside his house, the man began to doubt what he'd seen. He figured he simply had too much drink."

"And?"

"Next morning, he found deep scratch marks on his front door and something more…a scorched imprint of a horse's hoof."

"But he was safe, unharmed?"

Edward shook his head. "A week later, the man vanished—for good."

Hugo's story, Edward thought, was more valuable than drugs or alcohol. Lucie's face lost all its color. Her eyes darted back and forth between Edward and the swamp.

Edward pressed her arm. "We really should hurry."

As Lucie pulled him toward the car, he exaggerated his feigned limp. "Sorry, Lucie," he huffed. "Can't go any faster." He fished in his pocket. "Here." He presented her with the car key. "Go. Save yourself."

"And leave you here? No way am I going alone."

Edward limped to the car, sighing when they were inside with the doors locked. "Let's go." He accelerated the BMW down the gravel path as if the demons of hell were in hot pursuit. When the car reached the main road, Edward pulled onto the shoulder. He put his arm around Lucie and drew her close. "You okay, love?"

She leaned into his embrace. "Better now. But I'll be even better back at the inn."

Champagne, kissing, a massage perhaps, then... Edward grinned at his lustful thoughts, his mischievous eyes staring back at him in the car's rearview mirror.

Freshened with mouthwash and cologne, and palming two fresh condoms, Edward opened the bathroom door. The scene aroused him immediately. Light from the open door penetrated the darkness, arcing across the bed. Lucie's perfect alabaster skin looked as pure as fresh snow against dark-gray sheets. His reluctant goddess propped her head on two pillows. Her long, silky dark hair framed her young, supple breasts. A bottle of champagne and their close encounter with the supernatural were ideal aphrodisiacs.

Edward glanced from the motorway to Lucie, who again sat in the passenger seat of his BMW as the car raced east from Brussels through the Flemish countryside. She didn't appear to be the same naïve girl he pursued and then tricked into his bed so easily twelve weeks before. She had confidence, maturity. He didn't know if he found her transformation an attraction or a threat. He was, at once, aroused and frightened. "You're a woman of mystery, that's for sure."

Lucie scoffed. "A smart woman keeps the men guessing."

He squeezed her thigh. "Thrilled me to no end to get your text. But I'm a bit surprised that you suggested recreating our Limburg weekend."

"That weekend left an indelible mark on me. I thought it only fitting we try to reconcile where it all began, so to speak."

Edward felt smug. That Lucie wanted to have sex again didn't surprise him. He knew he was good in bed, though no woman had ever mentioned his *indelible mark*. No, he was surprised that she forgave him for what he had said in the car at the end of their weekend, on their drive back to Brussels. He was frank and, yes, even a bit callous, given her sexual surrender. But he thought it best not to string the poor girl along. Ingénue types were often clingy. So, as the car sped toward Brussels, Edward told Lucie that he didn't want to be tied down. He wanted an open relationship. As a matter of fact, he had a date that very night.

"Sorry you slapped me?" He assumed a playful tone although he was curious about her answer. He didn't want a repeat.

"No. You had it coming," she replied in a sassy tone. "Only sorry I couldn't hit you harder. You were speeding along the motorway and I didn't want to get myself killed."

Edward was relieved when Lucie let out a hearty laugh. Clearly, she'd put the episode behind her. However, he still didn't know one important fact. Had Lucie accepted his terms for their relationship or did she, like so many other women before her, think she could change him? That answer could wait. Before him stood a shared room at the Duke of Brabant Inn and a weekend of great makeup sex.

"Sorry, miss," the innkeeper said, "I know when you phoned, you specifically told my wife you wanted a single room with a double bed. All we have left are two singles, the same rooms you good people had on your last stay with us. Hate to disappoint repeat customers. Tell you what, I won't charge you more."

"Well, I should say not…given that this is all your fault." Lucie cast a sideways glance at Edward and rolled her eyes.

Her spunk surprised him, but he didn't want the weekend scuttled before the fun began. A narrow bed wouldn't thwart him. *It didn't prove an insurmountable impediment on my last visit with Lucie*, he thought. *Hell, some of my best sex happens on the bedroom floor.* "It's okay, sweetie. Let's take the two rooms."

Edward saw the surrender in her eyes before she nodded her agreement. She returned her attention to the contrite innkeeper. "I expect some other considerations as well. Bottle of champagne, perhaps?"

"As much as you fine folks can drink."

Upstairs in Edward's room, the couple polished off an entire bottle of champagne in no time. Edward thought Lucie was rather adept at refilling his empty glass. He surprised himself by declining her offer of opening a second bottle. She'd obviously gotten over the entire Schoverik legend as well. To prove that she had swept that prior weekend out of her head, she threw open the window of Edward's room and screamed, "Hey, Schoveriks, come out, come out wherever you are." She whistled several times before Edward pulled her from the window. "You'll get us arrested for disturbing the peace," *or worse, thrown out of the inn before we....*

Unsteady on her feet and limp in his arms, Lucie gazed up into his face. Her words began to slur. "If you don't mind, Edward dear, Edward, I'm going to go…to my room… now for a…nap, now. Feel…a bit…dizzy."

He didn't mind. He too felt a bit off-balance. He could use a nap himself before their big night. Lucie had booked a table at the same posh restaurant as before. And, what a coincidence, another full moon. After Lucie left, he fell backward onto the bed, lulled to sleep by fantasies of the evening and long night ahead.

What the hell was that? Edward batted open his eyes. The room and sky outside were dark. He must have slept for an hour, maybe longer. He reached for his phone on the nightstand when he heard, again, the sounds of neighing and heavy clomping hooves. *A horse?* Not uncommon in the country, but the noise was close. Rubbing his sleepy eyes, he hobbled to the window. He couldn't believe it. A massive black stallion stood in the yard below. But what grabbed his attention was the horse's rider. Edward squinted to make sure what he saw was real, and not a product of too much champagne. But the *thing*, for certainly it wasn't human, was still there—a ball of fire hovering above the horse.

Running downstairs, he found the innkeeper behind the bar. The affable fellow had resumed his role as barman, pouring out beers for two local residents.

Edward panted his question. "You…you chaps…see…and hear that?"

"See and hear what?" one of the men replied.

"A…a horse and…fireball."

The men looked at each other. Fear and concern swept across their faces. He swore one of them mouthed, "Schoverik."

"We didn't hear anything," the innkeeper said. "Doesn't mean those things weren't there. Just that they didn't come for us."

"You're not implying that they came for *me*?" The three men stared at him in silence. "I…I wasn't the one who whistled. It was her, Lucie." His gaze wandered to the beamed ceiling.

Lucie, she must have heard it. Edward ran back upstairs and knocked on her door. Lucie barely cracked open the door when he spoke, panic in his voice. "You hear the horse?"

Tilting her head, Lucie narrowed her eyes on him. "Are you okay?"

He pointed over her shoulder to the window, his arm shaking. "You must have heard the horse. It was there, just outside."

She shook her head slowly. "Been sitting in front of the makeup mirror for the past thirty minutes. Haven't heard a thing." She grabbed his trembling hand, steadying it against her chest. "Too much champagne, perhaps?"

He rubbed his temple. *Was it my imagination, or am I going crazy?* "Could be. Yes, that's probably it."

Lucie nudged him gently from her door. "Hurry up and get ready, sweetie. Reservation's for nine. We've got a long night ahead of us."

Why had he insisted on returning to the swamp? Was it his idea or Lucie's power of suggestion? Pre-dinner cocktails, a second bottle of wine, and the single-malt digestive clouded his memory. He convinced himself that he had to face his fear. It was irrational. Schoverik simply didn't exist.

He didn't argue with Lucie when she insisted on driving. After all they drank, she seemed remarkably sober, definitely more focused and self-assured than during that prior weekend. He was surprised that she found the gravel road, the same hidden lane he sought out on their last visit. And as he had done three months prior, she maneuvered his BMW down the narrow lane until they reached the dead-end. Before them loomed the trail that led to the high embankment and, beyond that, the ghoulish cesspool.

Edward stared out the car's side window, a sense of dread rising from the pit of his stomach, already queasy from the rich food and abundant drink.

"This ought to be fun," Lucie said, squeezing his thigh.

How can she be so chipper? "Couldn't we just stay here?"

Her response came in the form of a deep laugh as she opened her car door.

This time Lucie took the lead. She guided Edward through the forest, the air chilled by an October breeze, the trail beneath their feet softened by layers of fallen leaves. Grabbing his hand, she dragged him up the hill, dismissing his objections of ruining his new Italian shoes and trousers. Atop the embankment, the scene was much as he remembered. He didn't think it possible, but the onset of fall made the landscape bleaker. Mist rose from the murky water, swirling in the cool night air. Putrid smells of sulfur and sewer gas were even more pungent than on their first visit.

He turned his back to the swamp. "Okay, let's go."

"Not so fast, tiger."

"Huh?"

Lucie caressed his chest and nuzzled his neck. He noticed, for the

WILL-O'-THE-WISP

first time, the blanket nested beneath her arm, which she threw to the ground. "Let's both conquer our fears," she said, taking a step backward and removing her jacket. She nodded for him to do the same.

"I...I don't think this is such a good idea. We have that lovely bed back at the inn. Or even the car."

"You afraid of the Schoverik?"

"Not at all." He let out a wild whistle. He wanted to assert his manhood, prove that he wasn't scared. He also wanted to frighten Lucie as he did last time, to make her seek the safety of the car.

But she didn't flinch. Instead, she stroked his cheek. "Afraid of me then?"

"Certainly not!"

"Well, turn around while I ready myself. Get undressed. Or do you want me to do it?"

He did as he was told and began to disrobe. After he took off his jacket and dress shirt, a shrill wolf whistle came from behind him. *Lucie!* "Very funny. I assume by your whistle, then, you're ready." There was no answer. "Are you ready? Lucie—Lucie?"

Concerned by her silence, he turned. She was gone. *The Schoverik, have they snatched her?* He shook the thought from his head. "Schoverik are silly nonsense," he muttered aloud as if trying to convince himself. But the fact remained, Lucie was gone. "Lucie," he yelled repeatedly. But there was no answer. He gazed through the naked forest toward the car, its glossy finish glistening in the moonlight. The car was exactly as they'd left it.

He groaned. "Damn it! The car, the bloody car."

Lucie had the key. He was stuck miles from the nearest town. As he bent down to retrieve his discarded clothes, his eyes wandered to the distance, to the spot where the giant willows bent to kiss the swamp. That's when he saw them, just as he remembered—fireballs the size of men's heads. About a dozen of them, glowing, sparking—alive.

"Lucie," he bellowed again. "This isn't funny. Where the hell are you?"

Edward had to find her. He started to descend the embankment in the direction of the swamp but hesitated. He looked again toward the creatures in the distance. "Only marsh gas," he repeated to himself.

He gasped. Was it his imagination, or were they moving toward him? He tried to shake the thought from his mind with forced humor, but the chuckle that squeaked from his throat was more of a soft rattle.

He recalled the last time he'd spoken about the Schoverik, after his and Lucie's first encounter with the haunting spirits. It was at the inn, the morning after he used the macabre phenomenon to scare the tipsy Lucie into his bed. His ego had urged him to share the ingenious scheme with someone, anyone. He found Donald Pratcher, the university professor's brother, at the bar. From the man's lecherous remarks of the prior evening, Edward sized him up as a kindred spirit. Both men roared with laughter at Edward's tale of lust and conquest until that scowling prude, Dr. Chamberlain, appeared for breakfast.

Now twelve weeks later, alone in the nippy and foul forest air amid the Schoverik, Edward stood with his dark thoughts. Why was his former rowdy laugh escaping him? He stiffened. Was that the hair on the back of his neck standing? Were those goose bumps? He heard the neighing of a horse. Surely it was the very same beast he'd spotted under his window at the inn. He looked toward the sound but didn't see anything. Was it because the black stallion was as dark as the night?

The animal's shrill neighs came closer. Edward wasn't about to stand still. As he prepared to flee, he fell, twisting his ankle. Yelping in pain, he dropped to his knees. He began to roll down the hill. Momentum carried him closer and closer to the swamp. He looked skyward, gasping at the sight. Charging along the hill's ridge, less than a hundred yards away, was the mighty black beast. Steam escaped its nostrils. And atop the steed, a ball of fire.

Edward wailed, "Schoverik!"

Several days later, two hikers came across a man's Italian loafer beside the swamp. Police who searched the area found a blanket and

WILL-O'-THE-WISP

an abandoned black BMW. They traced the car's registration plate back to an Edward Crane, a British national and executive for a well-known Brussels-based distributor of religious giftware. Neither the car nor its owner, however, had been reported as missing.

A year later, Lucie and Hugo welcomed twins, a boy and girl. They named them Michael and Gudula, patron saints of the cathedral of Brussels. The couple wanted a symbolic nod to the place where they had met, the gift shop in the cathedral.

The couple's chance meeting was serendipitous, leading to a whirlwind romance and a collaboration of sweet, if not fiendishly clever, revenge. Hugo later confessed to Lucie that he noticed, at once, the beautiful woman who managed the gift shop. But it was her intelligence, kindness, and strong spirit that most attracted him.

Hugo had brought Dr. Chamberlain and her party to the cathedral at the conclusion of his Church and Folklore tour. Inside the gift shop, he introduced himself to Lucie, mentioning his home village of Diepenbeek. Her interest was piqued. When Hugo added that residents were known as Schoverik, Lucie replied that she knew all about them.

Having overheard their charming exchange, Dr. Chamberlain's brother Donald butted in. With a lecherous smirk on his face, he said he wanted to share something, "one helluva good story." Donald Pratcher proceeded to describe his chance encounter in Diepenbeek with a fellow traveler, "a slick womanizer" who boasted of an elaborate scheme in which he seduced a "pretty and clueless little thing" into his bed. Lucie listened with great interest.

This abrasive man's story about the Schoverik and the reluctant virgin, Lucie thought, *is more valuable than a tearful confession.*

Parvis de Saint-Gilles

Nigel Escott hurried across the nearly deserted parvis. The lead-colored sky that descended upon the city that early September day brought with it an incessant drizzle sufficient to sour the spirits of those with the sunniest of temperaments. Even on his best days, Nigel would never be mistaken for sunny. His disposition generally hovered somewhere in the twilight. After the paper-thin soles of his loafers sloshed into a puddle, he cursed, "Bloody Belgian climate!"

Nigel's pace quickened over the paving stones as he neared his destination. A glance at the clock on the church steeple indicated a few minutes before nine. He took comfort thinking that his favorite table and morning newspapers would be awaiting him. His hand patted the front pocket of his worn blue trousers. No, he hadn't forgotten his change. He'd scavenged enough coins from the top drawer of the bureau for a couple of coffees and a croissant. Flicking water from his green safari jacket, he dashed into the Maison du Peuple.

Although the parvis contained many cafés, the Maison du Peuple, or MDP, as locals called it, was certainly the most popular. The ambience was more reminiscent of the hipster coffeehouses of Amsterdam, New York, and London than the staid, traditional cafés of Paris or Brussels. Young entrepreneurs bought and transformed the MDP into a trendy hangout that attracted a mix of artists, writers, journalists, and self-employed consultants from the bohemian commune of Saint-Gilles. On weekend evenings, live performers and specialty disc jockeys molded the café's brand and grew its customer base. Whereas the Maison du Peuple had a decidedly youthful tilt at night, the café served a wider demographic during the morning and lunch hour. Inside, one was likely to hear more than a dozen languages. On market days, the carnival atmosphere of a bustling parvis spilled into the MDP.

As Nigel made his way to the long wooden bar, he scanned the room. Among the patrons, many with eyes glued to computer screens, he recognized only a smattering of faces. But it was still early. Gazing at the shelf of foreign-language newspapers, he was in luck—early enough to get *The Times of London* and *El Pais*, the Spanish daily. With papers in hand, he took a temporary perch on a barstool to place his order. "*Un café et un croissant, s'il vous plait.*"

After carefully counting out the dozen or so coins needed to make three euros for the breakfast special, he scanned *The Times*. Although he'd lived on the Continent for nearly three decades and hadn't set foot on British soil in several years, he considered England his home. His aged father, well over ninety years old, and two older brothers with whom Nigel had been estranged for years still lived in London.

Nigel shook his head at the headline warning of cataclysmic deficits plaguing the National Health Service. "Catastrophe," he mumbled to himself. Another article detailed an uptick in activity at the Calais refugee camp dubbed "The Jungle." Recent weeks had seen a spike in attempts by asylum seekers huddled in the French port to hop aboard lorries destined for the United Kingdom. Nigel didn't have an answer to the refugee question, but he was sympathetic to the plight of those fleeing homelands to seek a better life. "As long as they assimilate to Western values," he added when defending his position in conversations with others.

A pouty-faced server slid a cup of creamy coffee and a basket containing a croissant across the bar. Nigel offered a perfunctory "*Merci.*" With a raised eyebrow, the server silently scooped the change into his palm and turned to the register. Nigel merely shook his head. The MDP had been his morning ritual since relocating to Brussels three years before. But with rare exception, staff treated him like a stranger. He didn't feel singled out, however. Staff treated most customers with a mix of aloofness and disdain, reserving collegial banter for fellow workers. Nigel wondered whether surliness and sneers were prerequisites for a job, maybe even part of the café's hipster allure. Or, perhaps, indifference was merely a trait of the younger generation. It wasn't the same when he was a teenager, forty-odd years before, waiting tables on holidaymakers in Brighton, or so he believed.

Nigel tucked the newspaper under his arm and grabbed the basket and coffee. He liked the tables at the front of the café. Tall windows that reached to the lofty ceiling captured what scant natural light existed in Brussels. On either side of the entrance, long banquettes with cushions lined walls of exposed brick. One wall featured a colorful mural, a tropical scene with Gauguin-inspired women, palm trees, a volcano, and coffee beans. The café's logo, its initials outlined in purple, graced the opposite wall. In between, simple wooden tables covered an expansive planked floor.

Nigel preferred the banquettes. Others did too. These seats were the first to fill when the café opened at half past eight. Nigel's favorite spot nearest the window, under the tropical mural, was still vacant. After putting his breakfast down, he draped his damp coat on the straight-backed chair. He slid onto the cushioned bench and opened the newspaper. It was just a matter of time, he knew, before the café would fill to the brim. He gazed at the empty table on his right. He and other regular patrons understood that it was implicitly reserved for an elderly couple, native *Bruxellois*, by the looks of them.

As if on cue, the man and woman, both tall and lean, tottered in. Their vacant eyes and stone-faced expressions repelled greetings and chitchat. From observation, Nigel knew the white-haired couple's daily routine. They drank coffee in silence, side by side on the banquette, their backs to the wall. With chin raised and face void of expression, the woman surveyed the scene as the man stooped over a Belgian newspaper. They didn't converse with others and seldom spoke to each other. The couple lingered only until the man finished the newspaper, after which time their prime table became fair game. A couple of years before, Nigel had witnessed a short, friendly exchange in French between the couple and another elderly man who wandered into the MDP. But that was the extent of his glimpse into their lives.

Renzo Gatti tapped Nigel's table as he often did on entering the café. "*Buongiorno*, Signor Escott."

Nigel looked up from his paper and nodded at the man in the wrinkled denim shirt and baggy trousers. He considered Renzo an acquaintance, as many regulars in the café were, but nothing more. Nigel noticed the cane. His eyes dropped to the floor. One of the man's feet was wrapped in a bandage and set in therapeutic boot. "What happened to you?"

An avid cyclist, Renzo explained that a Brussels motorist who took the "right-turn priority" rule quite literally plowed his Fiat into him on Avenue Louise. "Good thing the driver wasn't German," Renzo added. "A BMW or Mercedes would have meant curtains. The Fiat fared far worse than this Italian." Renzo's deep laugh informed Nigel that the man wasn't terribly hurt.

"We'll talk later." Renzo hobbled off to fetch a coffee from the bar before taking his usual seat on the banquette on the other side of the elderly Belgian couple.

Nigel gazed out the window. Another acquaintance made his morning trek across the parvis. Before Michael Bergeron stepped into the Maison du Peuple, he shook the rain from his cap. Thinning blond hair and a high forehead made him look older than his forty years. Above a weak chin that anchored his long face were thin lips below light-blue eyes set too close together. A large nose was his noblest feature. In the time Nigel knew him, Michael never spoke of a romantic interest. He mentioned only a mother in Quebec.

Nigel watched with amusement as Michael blocked the café's exit to wipe rain splatters from his wire-rimmed glasses. He was oblivious to the sneer and mumbled curses of a café employee on his way outside for a smoke. Once inside, Michael dropped his shoulder bag onto an empty table. He made eye contact with Nigel, who responded with a silent nod.

After the elderly couple completed their morning ritual, Michael would relocate and take their vacated table between his two acquaintances. Nigel, Renzo, and Michael waited until that time to share news, gossip, activities, and misadventures. This had been the trio's routine for the past three years.

The elderly couple rose slowly from their seats. After a few moments steadying their balance, they put on their coats in silence. Nigel watched as Michael closed the Paris newspaper and grabbed his jacket. He crossed the café to claim his customary spot but a young woman with long blonde hair cut him off. Michael froze, a look of shock on his narrow face. Stirring up a cloud of jasmine-scented perfume, the woman swung her bag onto the banquette between Nigel and Renzo. Without acknowledging either man, she placed a cup of hot tea and a pastry on the empty table. Nigel reckoned she was no more than thirty. Her clothes were urban chic and she had an air of confidence about her that intrigued him.

Michael remained at a standstill, the look of shock on his face turning to annoyance. Renzo and Nigel stared at the woman. Removing a laptop from her bag, she seemed oblivious to having disrupted the natural order of things at the Maison du Peuple. Nigel was already plotting to get the pretty young thing into his bed. He feared that Renzo might intercede on Michael's behalf. *Whoever speaks first*, Nigel thought, *will seal the Canadian's fate.*

After smoothing the front of his rumpled shirt, Nigel tried to get the woman's attention by clearing his throat. When that didn't

PARVIS DE SAINT-GILLES

work, he added, "Dreadful weather we're having at the moment." The Englishman's uncharacteristic smile, tilt of his head, and exaggerated Oxbridge accent were his trademark tactics to charm the opposite sex.

With a chest-heaving sigh, Michael stormed away to reclaim his former seat.

Nigel repeated his climatic observation in a louder voice, hoping to break the ice on the second attempt.

The young woman shrugged. "I'm used to it. Seattle's home."

Nigel's expression showed surprise. "American? Don't get many of your countrymen, or should I say countrywomen, in these parts. Welcome, welcome. My name's Nigel."

"English," she said more as a statement than a question. Accepting his hand, she introduced herself as Jenny Stein. "I'm a journalist. Freelancer. Here to do a series on refugees."

"Well then, Brussels is the place to be. The bureaucrats will have it all figured out, mark my words."

Jenny laughed. Nigel laughed too.

"That's just it," she said, her tone filled with scorn. "Solutions will come from the front lines. They always do. In-your-face crisis demands action. The EU should be leading, but it won't." She pointed at Nigel's newspaper. "There, you see. Calais is a mess. The Greek Isles are a mess, the Balkans are a mess, and so on and so on."

Renzo's exaggerated cough got Nigel's attention. "Jenny, my apologies. There beside you is Renzo Gatti. Another Brussels wayfarer."

The American woman turned and shook hands with the Italian. "Pleased to meet you."

"We're regulars. Michael too," Renzo said, motioning across the café to the still-simmering French Canadian. "As a matter of fact, you've taken his spot."

"Oh, oh. I didn't know. I'm so sorry. I can move." Jenny made an effort to shut her laptop.

Catching Jenny's hand, Nigel shot Renzo a nasty look. "There

— 139 —

are no reserved seats. You're welcome to sit anywhere. We're all just migrant birds. Folks who live around the parvis get a bit too territorial, that's all."

"By the way, what is a parvis?"

Nigel sat up, puffing out his chest. He enjoyed dispensing facts. "A parvis is an open enclosed space."

Jenny looked at Nigel over her *pain au chocolat*. "I thought it meant *place*, like in the Grand Place."

"Ah, yes, common mistake. Parvis refers specifically to an area in front of a church or cathedral. I'm assuming you noticed the church at the top of the parvis. Neo-Roman, nineteenth century." Jenny nodded. Placing her elbow on the table, she rested her chin in her palm. "*Parvis* is derived from *paradise*," Nigel continued. "Has an ancient lineage—Persian, Greek, Latin. Original meaning is an enclosure."

Nigel felt Jenny study him with new respect. He assumed that his chances of bedding the woman were improving. With her back to Renzo, Jenny didn't notice the Italian roll his eyes. With a shake of his head, Renzo turned his attention back to the Italian newspaper.

"So, what brings you here—"

"*Nigel*, Nigel," he repeated, sensing her struggle to recall his name. "Left England thirty years ago. Followed a lovely señorita to Barcelona. Marriage soured, followed shortly thereafter by my business. Made my way here three years ago. The rest is a long story. I won't bore you. Suffice it to say, Brussels is comparatively inexpensive as European capitals go. Not the best place I've lived; not the worst either."

"I think it's charming, Nigel. So much history, beautiful architecture, interesting people. As a journalist, I find the city ripe with stories at the moment. I'll grab what I can, then off to Hungary in a couple of days."

Nigel nodded. He recognized her genuine exuberance. Everything Americans touched in Europe was *darling, quaint,* or *charming*—even if it was made in China. He didn't object. As a matter of fact, it gave him certain advantages with the ladies. "Brussels has its charms. But it's a bit like *Casablanca*." The woman's puzzled expression prompted him to add, "You have seen the film?"

"Of course. Bogart and Bergman, two of my favorites. But the connection to Brussels?"

Nigel craned his head around the café before returning his gaze to Jenny. "We're all waiting for the Lisbon plane."

"Lisbon plane?"

Nigel explained that most of the expats he encountered viewed Brussels as a way station. "All have plans or, at the very least, dreams of moving on. Maybe that's why the Belgians keep to themselves. They see the rest of us as mere transients."

Nigel gestured toward Renzo, who stood at the bar ordering another coffee. "Take him. Left Italy two decades ago. Fled the seminary. Or was he expelled? Doesn't really matter. Considers himself lucky to have escaped the Catholic Church before it smothered him. Renzo's a free spirit. Gallivanted around Europe before getting stuck in Brussels six years ago."

"Stuck, or maybe happy to settle down?"

"You can ask him, but Renzo's always going on about returning to his beloved Roma."

Nigel didn't tell Jenny everything about Renzo. The Italian was a player. He used his accent and modest income from an inherited annuity to seduce men into his bed. He didn't have a type, as far as appearance went anyway. Pretty boys and scruffy-faced hooligans were equal prey. Desperation, loneliness, and hunger were the shared traits of his conquests. "Trouble with Rome," Renzo had once said to Nigel, "not only is it expensive, it's loaded with Italians. How's a man supposed to use a sexy accent to his advantage?"

Nigel nodded across the café. His other acquaintance sipped coffee while banging away at a laptop. "Take Michael over there. Earned the right to live and work in the EU through his mother, an émigrée from Paris to Montreal. He's an IT expert, a specialist in Internet security. Books and travel are his thing. Gets work here and there until he saves enough for his next exotic adventure. Been to Sri Lanka, Thailand, and Botswana just since I've known him. Finds Brussels boring. Tired of it, as a matter of fact."

"His dream?"

"Living in Paris. But distaste for full-time employment makes that more of a fantasy than an achievable goal—even if he doesn't see that himself."

"And you? Are you also waiting for the Lisbon plane?"

Nigel took a deep breath. His fingers tapped his chin. A glint flickered in his brown eyes. "Already got my ticket."

Her cup paused midway between the table and her lips. "Really?"

Nigel nodded, a look of satisfaction swept across his face. "Several irons in the fire, as a matter of fact." Nigel described projects ranging from inventions to screenplays to smart-phone applications. But his primary focus was the launch of a charter airline in Spain. "If all goes well, I'll be back in Spain by Christmas."

"Barcelona?"

Nigel's lips formed a sly grin. "Perhaps."

Nigel hurried across the nearly deserted parvis. The lead-colored sky that descended upon the city that early March brought with it an incessant drizzle. After his loafers, their soles now riddled with holes, sloshed into a puddle, he cursed, "Bloody Belgian climate!"

He stood at the bar to order a coffee and croissant. After counting out his change, he ogled the figure of the new female server making his drink. Dismissing her as a lesbian, he grabbed *The Times of London* and *El Pais* before making his way to his usual table. He greeted Renzo with a simple "Good morning." The Italian was already seated on the banquette sipping coffee and reading *la Repubblica*, the Italian daily. A bicycle helmet rested on the table.

Renzo flashed a broad grin and glanced over to where Michael was poring over his newspaper. "Should be back in Roma before Easter. I'll fill in the details when Michael joins us."

Nigel replied with a faint smile. It wasn't the first time Renzo spoke with zeal of returning to Rome. And despite Renzo's confident tone that suggested otherwise, Nigel suspected it wouldn't be the last time. Some hurdle usually surfaced. More often than not, Renzo's excuse for staying in Brussels had to do with a fresh infatuation or an overdrawn bank account.

Nigel spread out the newspaper and sipped his coffee. Refugee stories filled the front page with the European Union pledging unified action. The new U.K. prime minister declared as top priorities the rescue of the struggling National Health Service and a solution to the overcrowded Calais refugee camp.

An hour or so later, Michael closed his newspaper. He shoved a travel brochure for Namibia into his satchel, gathering it and his jacket off the empty chair. As Nigel watched Michael zigzag among the tables, he wondered what might have happened to the elderly couple. It wasn't like them to skip a morning. Sometimes one or the other missed the daily ritual, but never both.

After depositing his belongings, Michael dropped onto the padded bench. He looked first to Nigel, then to Renzo. Each shrugged, silent replies indicating they didn't know the whereabouts of the missing couple.

Nigel sat up and squared his shoulders. "Well, I finished the screenplay. Sending it off to a Hollywood agent. All goes well, I'll be in Barcelona by Christmas."

"Congratulations," Michael said. "And here I thought I had the day's best morsel."

"Oh, what's that?" Renzo asked.

"A new job."

"Paris?" asked Nigel.

Renzo and Nigel looked at Michael with anticipation. He

swallowed hard; a blush crossed his cheek. "No. Antwerp. I'll commute two days a week. Rest of the time, I'll be right here," he added with a tap to the tabletop.

Nigel and Renzo nodded slowly when an elderly man caused a stir at the café's door. The man had tripped on the threshold. He stopped a nasty tumble to the floor by catching the edge of a table. The table's startled patrons stood as their spilled coffee streamed to the floor.

After a lengthy absence, Nigel returned to his seat carrying another coffee. He looked more sullen than usual. "Disturbing news, I'm afraid."

Responding to his acquaintances' puzzled looks, he gestured back to the bar. There, the old guy who had stumbled into the café sat on a stool, his expression dazed. He sipped coffee using both hands to steady a shaking cup.

"The old couple, the ones who always sit here," Nigel said, tapping Michael's table. "Dead. Double suicide. Or maybe just a tragic coincidence. No one knows for sure."

Michael and Renzo gasped.

Nigel continued, "They've been coming here for years, the old chap said, before it was the Maison du Peuple. Not even husband and wife. Brother and sister. Orphaned during the war. Lived together on the parvis ever since."

"Their names?" asked Michael.

"Huh?"

"Their names. They have names?"

Nigel shook his head. "No one seems to know. Guess I could check out the mailbox." Responding to their blank stares, he added, "They lived in my building…for more than sixty years. Imagine that."

Nigel's gaze wandered out the window to the rain-soaked parvis. A feeling of dismay, even sadness swept over him as he considered the fact that he never knew that the two people who sat beside him nearly every morning for the past three and a half years lived a solitary existence just one floor above him. *And now they're gone.*

After a wistful sigh, Nigel pushed the thought from his head and lowered himself onto the bench. With heads down, the three men sat in silence, their expressions sullen. One by one, they returned to their coffees and newspapers.

Nigel turned the page of *The Times of London*. A byline caught his eye, a familiar name, Jenny Stein. "Well I'll be," he muttered aloud as he read the headline of her article: "Waiting for the Lisbon Plane."

The Ginger Cat

*A**gain, that blasted tapping*. Still, Peter Favell didn't lift his nose from the book. He sank lower into the supple leather cushions of his Chesterfield sofa. His long legs stretched forward to a rustic coffee table on which his stockinged feet came to rest. Without the commitments of family, a Sunday afternoon in Brussels offered few diversions except a walk, a drink, or a drive. But even Peter could absorb only so much drizzle, beer, and flat green countryside. Weekends were when he missed his ex-boyfriend the most. Their three-year romance had ended months before, when Martin decided that love in the Low Countries was no substitute for a posh flat and a fab life in London. Peter's heart was still too wounded for him to consider another relationship.

Peter had spent two hours the prior morning scanning the shelves of Waterstones bookstore. In the end, book jacket testimonials drove his purchase of the latest winner of the Royal Literary Award. The thin novel told the story of a trio of average blokes who reconnect at a funeral after a thirty-year separation. A tale of secrets and unfulfilled ambitions set amid the decay of Liverpool spoke to Peter's sullen mood.

Dismissing the irregular tapping sounds as by-products of his flat's ancient heating system, Peter made an extra effort to focus through a dense patch of the book's narrative. But the tapping kept vexing his concentration. That the building constructed in the nineteenth century wasn't more solid surprised him. The walls, a combination of paneled wood and beige plaster accented with dove-gray framing, suggested fashionable gentility. The sounds emanating through the walls, however, were more coarse than refined: screaming moans of an old man, clattering of dishes from the restaurant that abutted Peter's kitchen, dashes of toddlers up the stairs of the neighboring building. The ceiling wasn't discreet either. Its thin layer of plaster revealed the secrets of his new neighbor, a lead-footed woman from Paris whose two daughters plunked away on the keys of an out-of-tune piano. Peter knew her name only from a plate on the mailbox. The nightly barrage of noise convinced Peter that Madame Desbarats spent her evenings rearranging the furniture and bouncing a ball for her yappy little white dog. He missed her predecessor, a quiet woman who worked for the Swiss embassy. Too efficient and too Swiss for a pet, she rearranged her furniture merely once in a fortnight.

Peter got used to the constant reshuffling of neighbors and the fact that he was probably the only Brit living in the building. Brussels was, after all, a city of expats. Besides the usual cadre of consultants, bankers, and corporate executives who inhabited most major cities, the gloomy capital was home to NATO and thirty thousand bureaucrats of the European Union. Every other car, it seemed to Peter, bore a number plate beginning with CD, the prefix that denoted *Corps Diplomatique*. Perhaps he was merely jealous. Peter wished his own Audi 6, a car provided by his employer, a global pharmaceutical giant, carried the pretentious designator if, for nothing else, to impress the imaginary lovers about whom he sometimes fantasized on lonely evenings at home.

In his building, a stately four-floor stone townhouse that an investor had fashioned into seven flats, Peter counted a turnover of six neighbors during his two-year tenure. Occupying the ground floor, what the real-estate agent called the *rez-de-chaussée*, Peter had a great vantage point from which to observe his neighborhood. Three tall double windows in the front looked onto Rue d'Ecosse while the large walled garden at the back, his private oasis, gave Peter views into his neighbors' lives. The setting reminded him of Hitchcock's film, *Rear Window*. Peter took offense with Martin's calling him a 'voyeur,' although he understood his former lover offered the comment only in jest. "Might fit if I owned a pair of binoculars," Peter had replied, at the time, in his defense.

The city's constant churn was evident. New faces appeared on the street as familiar ones disappeared. One such face, an elderly man Peter nicknamed "the Professor," watched from the pavement opposite for hours as movers transferred Peter's household goods from their lorry into his flat. The bearded man wearing a black fedora and lavender scarf stirred Peter's interest, reminding him both of a favorite literature professor at Cambridge and a character from a Thomas Mann story. He thought he'd like to know him. But the Professor vanished within weeks of Peter's arrival, his death announced by a funeral wreath and a terse posting on the green door of number 16, a boarding house for pensioners.

The rat-a-tat-tats intensified, causing Peter to reread a passage of dialogue for a third time. The scene, a pub: three men gather after the funeral to toast their departed mate. The conversation pivots to self-reflection. A divorced man laments his life, "Each choice fastened another timber; every year drove another post. Now, the open gate's more annoyance than opportunity." Although only midway through the book, Peter reckoned that the dead mate was the character with the brightest future.

The wailing siren of an ambulance drew Peter's glance over his shoulder. That was when he noticed a woman at the window, her hand poised to tap the glass. Her thin pursed lips attempting a smile signaled relief that he'd finally seen her while dark piercing eyes and creased brow suggested frustration that he'd taken so bloody long to do so. He recognized the plain woman with short graying hair. She was a neighbor from up the street—number 18, 20, or maybe 22. They'd passed on the pavement, each toting plastic shopping bags to or from Delhaize. She was one of the few passersby who didn't turn, or worse,

THE GINGER CAT

sneer, when he offered a bonjour. In a city where smiles were as rare as sunshine, the smallest flash of familiarity was a welcome prize.

After jumping to his feet, Peter released the latch, pushed aside a stack of old books, and pulled open the window. The woman was visible only from the chest up, the rest of her body disappearing below the sill. He gazed down at her, offering a polite nod of his head. "Bonjour."

"Bonjour," the woman replied before rattling off some more words in French. All Peter deciphered was *yesterday* and *home*.

"*Anglais?*" he asked with a shrug. He knew enough French to survive an afternoon at the market or order a meal, but he was lost when the person replied in rapid-fire fashion.

"*Oui, oui,* yes, English." Her accent was thick. They exchanged names as she reached up to accept Peter's extended hand. Majori, as he now knew her, moved her palm to the base of her neck. "Were you… at home…*hier*…yesterday?"

"Yes. Part of the afternoon." After browsing through the bookstore in the morning, Peter had spent much of the day checking out gay bars in Antwerp by himself.

Majori's face lit up. "Then maybe you saw?"

Peter cocked his head. "Saw?"

"*Oui.* I was robbed."

Peter flinched. "Robbed? Really. I'm so very sorry."

Majori launched into her tale. "Man, Moroccan, maybe Turk… ripped gold chain…right off me." Her hand slid down from her neck revealing a thin line of red skin. "Yesterday afternoon. Just after lunch. Maybe you see?"

Peter shook his head slowly from side to side. "Terribly sorry. I'd gone by then. I drove over to Antwerp, um…with a mate."

He saw the disappointment on her face. An exasperated sigh blew through her pressed lips. He felt awful that he couldn't offer assistance. Without prodding, Majori shared an expanded version of the story. "Lived here for thirty years. Nothing like this has ever happened." Returning from the supermarket, she and her husband had paused outside their building to unlock the door. As she turned the doorknob, a young man lunged at them. He shoved Majori's eighty-year-old husband across the threshold and onto the ground. As she went to her husband's aid, the attacker tore the gold chain from her neck.

"He ran this way, right past your window." A pained expression suggested she was reliving the moment. She looked again into Peter's face almost as if hoping the new details might jog his memory. Her distress begged for aid. But Peter wasn't home. He saw nothing.

"Went that way," she added, pointing toward Rue de Bosquet. "I ran after him but lost him in the Metro."

Her shoulders and chin lifted. It was clear to Peter that Majori wore the ordeal like a badge of honor. Although she didn't seem old enough, *Majori,* he thought, *would have been a star of the Belgian resistance.* After saying goodbye with sympathetic words and a final handshake, Peter watched the woman amble up the street looking into other ground-floor windows in search of witnesses.

Over the next few days, Peter noticed more police patrols on the streets around his home. But soon they disappeared. During his two years living at number 4, he had witnessed several staggering drunks, smashed car windows, and the occasional beggar, but never a mugging or an assault. He figured if he ignored the panhandlers and avoided eye contact with the beer-reeking vagrants, he'd be fine.

Michel, the short, amiable man who sold sandwiches and coffee from a nearby storefront on weekdays, was full of stories. He told Peter that the Slovenian couple at number 6 were recent victims of a break-in. "Then there was your former upstairs neighbor," Michel added. "Swiss lady. Robbed as she slept. Thief got in from the terrace…above your kitchen. Took her purse and phone. Thankfully…nothing else."

Peter dismissed the crimes as hazards of living in the city center.

His six-foot husky frame, he figured, made him an unlikely target anyway. Despite the crime and unsavory street characters, he liked his neighborhood, the section of Saint-Gilles where bohemian commune met upmarket Ixelles and Place Louise. A five-minute walk in one direction brought Peter to the front doors of Tiffany, Versace, and Dior. Five minutes in the other delivered him to the Parvis. The large square was home to a photogenic little church into which Peter never set foot. The square also housed a market, vegan restaurants, shabby bars, and tired cafés known for inexpensive coffee, surly wait staffs, and an eclectic clientele of artists, writers, and pensioners. Among the cafés, a social services center served a diverse clientele of street people including a few he'd seen mumble to themselves. Except for one unprovoked confrontation involving an imagined slight, Peter didn't feel threatened. On the contrary, he was glad that those in need had a place to go for help.

A week after his window conversation with Majori, Peter poured his Monday morning coffee and walked to the front of the apartment. He hit the switch lifting metal security shutters that covered his windows. As daylight flickered into his sitting room, flashes of blue speckled the beige walls. Curiosity drew his eyes to the street.

Instead of the usual stream of cars that flowed up Rue d'Ecosse to commute into the city center, several blue and white cars of the Politie were parked haphazardly in the intersection. With lights flashing, they blocked access to the adjoining streets. Pressing nearer to the window, Peter observed that blue-uniformed police had cordoned off the entrance to an apartment block on the opposite side of the road. Anxious faces in windows of neighboring buildings peered at the scene. Pedestrians hustling to the Metro slowed, their glances trained on the police activity. With a cigarette in his hand, Michel stood at the edge of the yellow police tape chatting with a couple of policemen. Peter recognized the pair as regular patrons of the sandwich shop.

Peter drank a second cup of coffee while staring out the window.

An ambulance pulled up to number 9, its siren wailing. *Never a good sign,* he thought. Reluctantly, Peter pushed himself away from the window to shower and dress for work. He'd find out what happened later, from Michel, another resident of his building, or maybe never. *No good comes from sticking one's nose....*

Peter didn't have to wait for Michel or bother a neighbor to learn what happened. Walking home from the Metro after work, Peter found Rue d'Ecosse alive with activity. Several people congregated on the pavement opposite number 9. Tattered remnants of police tape dangled from the building's facade. Another piece lay in the gutter, an eviscerated jaundiced snake. If not for the morning's commotion, Peter might have mistaken the gathering for a block party. A few of the men drank from red Jupiler beer cans, and several squealing children played tag, darting between the adults' legs.

As he sidled up to the group, Peter noticed Majori, the only neighbor whose name he knew. He assumed the fragile man with the bandaged forehead, leaning on a cane, was her husband. As Peter edged next to Majori, voices in a mix of languages provided details. Peter's ears filtered out all but the English speakers among them.

"Murder for sure." A pencil-thin man attired entirely in gray said to a purple-haired woman who approached from the opposite direction.

"Frightening," she replied, leaning in to kiss his cheeks. "Michel will know. I'll ask him in the morning."

"Bah! Gotta be murder. Police wouldn't be here all day if it weren't," added a pot-bellied man in a rumpled suit. "Robbery for sure…or worse."

"Simply a matter of time," Majori said, before acknowledging Peter with a smile.

Peter attempted to enter the conversation. "Who was—"

THE GINGER CAT

But before he completed his question, answers popcorned in various accents from the huddle.

"*Nederlandse.*"

"Young…ish."

"Red *haar*…cat."

"Ginger…Daphne."

"Nice enough—"

"When her cat went missing and she needed…"

An image of the dead woman flashed into Peter's head. He wasn't certain whether the cat was named Daphne and its owner Ginger, or the other way around. Both had red hair and kept to themselves, except for the cat's occasional foray into his garden. Peter knew enough to ring at number 9 to inform Daphne whenever Ginger, *or was it the other way around,* got trapped in his garden. Their conversation never advanced beyond the roving cat. The young, heavily pierced woman with short-cropped hair who retrieved her cat was Dutch—that Peter knew—maybe even a lesbian, but on that point he wasn't sure.

The "tattooed cat lady from Amsterdam" was how he catalogued her. He had others: the German lady with a plump baby, the head-bobbing Italian woman with an elderly mother, the grumpy gay couple with a bulldog, the standoffish architect, the hot French lad in tight jeans. And until their recent introduction and mention of a husband, Majori had been the smiling spinster. In addition to Majori, the head-bobber and sneering architect were among the evening's crowd.

Majori turned to a stout, white-haired woman attired entirely in black. "Madame Geneste, didn't you complain to me, only yesterday, that her cat got into your garden again over the weekend? 'Maddening,' you said."

The woman who Peter thought lived and practiced psychology out of the gray stone house at number 8 seemed flustered. Her jowly cheeks crimsoned.

"W…w…well, yes," she stammered, glancing at the other faces. Peter felt a collective bristle, the slight recoil of the crowd away from the speaker as the group's sympathy flowed toward the recently deceased. "But I didn't complain," she added hastily. "Never called the police either. Not good for the cat, that's all. Even fed the poor creature."

The woman's final comment seemed to pacify the onlookers, who began the slow process of dispersing when a light drizzle began to fall. As the crowd broke up into smaller clusters, Peter caught snippets of conversations: "Cat's still missing." "Heard about a service at the chapel run by the Polish sisters." "Let's meet for drinks." "How about dinner some night?" "Walk her home." "Lock your doors."

Majori introduced Peter to her husband and a couple of other residents of her building. They seemed nice and even had proper names. The brooding hunk became Gerard, the duck-faced lap-dancer, Natalia. As Peter bade Majori and his new acquaintances good night, he recognized a couple who lived on an upper floor of his building. He scurried to catch up. After introducing themselves, the three walked toward the tall gray double doors of number 4, expressing sympathy for the dead woman.

"Takes tragedy to bring people together," the young husband said in a Scandinavian accent. The man's wife nodded and Peter muttered his agreement.

"See you around," Peter said before slipping into his flat.

The sandwich shop didn't open the next day or the day after that. Peter didn't know whether Michel lowered his shutters out of respect for the dead woman or because of some personal matter. Despite closure of the neighborhood's gathering place, the esprit de corps that sprouted among the residents of Rue d'Ecosse after the tragic death of the woman in number 9 blossomed. Peter had never heard so many hellos nor saw so many smiles as he walked to and from his home. Vagrants seemed fewer. Those who did wander into the neighborhood seemed less threatening. Peter took to dropping spare change into a beggar's cup on the way to the Metro. The old man's garbled "Merci" filled Peter with satisfaction, a connection, though slight, to his neighborhood.

A flyer turned up in Peter's mailbox announcing the woman's memorial service in a week's time. Leaving for work a few days later, Peter noticed a huddle of people around Michel's shop. While Peter made his way toward the gathering, the stout psychologist Madame Geneste seemed to hiss at him as she hurried away from the group, heading for her home.

"Suicide." He heard the word repeated among the crowd. He wasn't sure whether he detected surprise or disappointment in the tones.

His upstairs neighbor Madame Desbarats plodded toward him in the square-heeled boots he had heard but never seen before that morning. "Bonjour, Monsieur Favell. Poor girl died in the bathtub. Slit her wrists."

"Should be a great relief it's not murder," he said, nodding toward the huddle of people outside Michel's shop. "But they don't look happy."

With eyebrows raised, Madame Desbarats tilted her head from side to side. A smug grin formed on her lips. "The note," she said, as if that explained everything.

"A…suicide note?" he asked with hesitation in his voice.

The woman nodded. "*Oui, oui.* Suicide note." Madame Desbarats heaved a sigh. "Poor girl just wanted her cat."

"Her cat?"

"She felt alone, isolated. Unkind words for the neighbors, especially *that* one." Peter turned, following the woman's stare up the street. He was just in time to see the psychologist push her way through her front door and slam it shut.

Peter's gaze returned to his upstairs neighbor. "Did she name Madame Geneste?"

"Didn't have to." Madame Desbarats used her nose to motion at the crowd outside Michel's. "They all knew. Seems the old *vache* told Daphne she was calling animal control. Be done with the cat once and for all."

In the days that followed, life on Rue d'Ecosse slowly returned to the way it was before the death in number 9. Acquaintances made during days of bonding faded like an untended fire. People scurried passed each other with blank faces. The snake of police tape trapped in the gutter disintegrated further as a lorry came to collect the dead woman's belongings.

Peter altered his plans so that he could attend the memorial service. The tattooed cat lady he now knew as Daphne was one of the few neighbors with whom he had had any interaction, if only because of her wandering ginger cat. At the service, stern-faced Polish nuns in gray outnumbered the few neighbors in attendance. After a moment's hesitation, Peter sat next to the brooding hunk he now knew as Gerard. They exchanged a warm embrace.

A few weeks later, Daphne's missing cat turned up meowing at the door of number 9. A water dish and a bowl of food appeared on the sidewalk. One morning soon after, as Peter rushed to work, he noticed officers from animal control putting a cage with the tiny ginger cat into the back of a small blue lorry.

"Bastards."

Peter turned to see the speaker, the petite blonde wife of the Slovenian diplomat in number 6. The expression on Peter's face must have begged for an explanation.

"It's a *kill* shelter," she said, words seething from her lips before she turned from the scene in disgust.

As he stared at the lorry, Peter considered adopting the ginger cat. *But do I really want to be tied down? Maybe if things work out with Gerard, we could…* he thought. *Then again, might be a good companion.* "Ah," he muttered to himself, thinking about the cat's death sentence, "still have a couple days to decide."

And with that, Peter Favell, his head down, hurried along the rain-splattered pavement to the Metro station. Although his thoughts turned to the busy day ahead, he remembered to drop a couple of euros into the old beggar's cup.

Christmas Carousel

A freckle-faced boy squealed atop a yellow sea horse whose snout nudged an orange blowfish mounted by a giggling doll of a toddler. Mischievous twins poked each other inside the belly of a blue whale while other children screamed with delight as they straddled a feathery ostrich, green snail, flying goose, and cherry-red ladybug. These were just a few of the strange and fabulous creatures of *le manège du marché de Noël*.

"Fantastical" is what Elise Bertrand called the carousel, a popular feature of Brussels' annual Christmas market. A server in a nearby restaurant, Elise delighted in imagining the ride as something ripped from the pages of a fairy tale, the product of a wild and limitless imagination. Unbridled mirth produced by the whimsical merry-go-round flooded her with fond images of early childhood. Ah, but if only she could train her mind to erase what came later—the abrupt end of laughter, love, and innocence triggered by her beloved father's death.

At least she had help in suppressing her bad memories.

The arrival of the annual Christmas market in late November brought a vibrant throng of animated people. Along with the hordes of locals, tourists from all corners of the globe descended upon Sainte-Catherine, the Brussels neighborhood also known for its cluster of fish and seafood restaurants, and pubs brimming with young revelers. For six weeks at the end of the year, dozens of bright stalls offered ornaments, jewelry, candles, and other trinkets along with refreshment. The chilly air swirled with scents of candied almonds, roasted chestnuts, *vin chaud* (hot mulled wine), and *tartiflette,* a hardy French Alpine dish of potatoes, cheese, onions, bacon, and white wine served from enormous cast-iron skillets. The carnival atmosphere smothered inhibitions, erasing years of life and layers of weighty concerns among young and old, including Elise.

Then there were the vendors themselves—a diverse lot of colorful characters from near and far. The prior year had featured a group of Canadian merchants. In the shadow of the city's thirteenth-century Black Tower, they sold a variety of provincial products including snowshoes, bearskin hats, and maple syrup. A boy from Saskatchewan wooed Elise for the duration of the Christmas market. She simply wasn't ready to date, but she considered the persistent boy too sweet, too cute, too transitory to reject too harshly. By the time he returned to Saskatoon, his failed flirtations had cost him a small fortune in gifts of maple syrup, a stuffed polar bear, and boxes of kitschy chocolates marketed as peppermint moose droppings.

The corner seafood bar and restaurant where Elise worked was among the area's most popular on account of good, reasonably priced food and drink, a lively atmosphere, and an auspicious location. One side faced the bustling Place Sainte-Catherine, anchored by the square's namesake church, while the other opened onto a main thoroughfare lined with bars and cafés that led to Boulevard Anspach and the Grand Place.

Most weekends, and especially for the duration of the annual Christmas market, Elise and her co-workers barely caught their breaths. Boisterous patrons spilled into the streets, huddled around tall round tables. Others loitered in the square with a drink in one hand and a cigarette or oyster shell in the other. Laughter and the clinking of glasses rose above the clatter of eager forks picking at plates piled high with mussels, clams, shrimp, and other delicacies of the sea.

The frenetic pace wasn't the worst part of Elise's work; neither were the drunks nor the occasional nicks and gashes her hands suffered from shucking oysters and cracking crab legs. All of that, she understood, merely came with the job. And despite her best efforts to dress down, a sports cap, baggy wool trousers, and a chunky Nordic sweater didn't disguise her long, silky blonde hair and shapely figure enough to deter the overconfident loudmouths whom she rebuffed with icy poise. But even unwanted advances weren't the worst feature of her job.

No, Elise was annoyed by the most ordinary of things: numb fingers. Seafood, *fruits de mer*, literally, "fruits of the sea," required ice to remain fresh—lots and lots of ice. Fingerless gloves kept Elise's palms reasonably warm and allowed her to wipe a runny eye or a sniffling nose with the back of her hand. But relief for chilly fingers that turned the red of boiled lobster by the end of the night eluded her.

After one long shift, Elise returned to her small flat in Anderlecht. She stood at the kitchen sink holding her aching hands under the hot tap for what seemed an eternity. As was her custom, she let her gaze drift out the window, over the sill cluttered with spent wine bottles. She made a game of scanning the darkness for signs of the holiday season. A few strands of colored lights outlining doorways and snaking across balconies broke up the usual gloom of the long, dark Belgian winter. The appearance of a new *sapin de Noël*, or Christmas tree, in some neighbor's window always sparked her interest. She couldn't resist judging the merits of each new tree that debuted, both in terms of its natural beauty and the artificial adornments added by human hands. Her fascination was more than mere appreciation for the colorful evergreens themselves. Beyond the tree-filled windows, she imagined scenes of domestic bliss, places in the dark, lonely world where love, happiness, and hope still existed, even if they eluded her.

A bright blue star, almost phosphorescent, atop the most recent holiday tree to appear in her neighborhood tableau reminded her of the decorations in Sainte-Catherine. Large blue and silver stars suspended from wires strung between the square's many trees. Her mind wandered back to the Christmas market and the square's rowdy and playful crowd.

Everyone was in a jolly mood even before guzzling the white wine and champagne she served. She marveled at the endless streams of alcohol poured from bottles standing at the ready in stainless-steel troughs. Of course, the bottles also chilled on ice—lots and lots of additional ice. But despite many distractions that competed for her attention, Elise's thoughts kept returning to the carousel. The marvelous menagerie had an almost magnetic pull. Whether serving champagne or dishing up a plate of shrimp, Elise couldn't resist gazing across the square.

Each Christmas, as if the magical beasts tired of their human handler, someone new operated the ride. To be fair, Elise reasoned, her perspective was limited. She'd observed only three of the annual markets and three operators. But each carousel boy was indeed very different from the other, as unique as the merry-go-round's exotic creatures themselves. She didn't know why, but the current boy in charge of the fantastical ride mesmerized her.

Boy!

The object of her curiosity was probably a man, a young man, but definitely not a boy. Having turned twenty-one earlier in the year, Elise bristled whenever a customer brought attention to her youthfulness. However, she couldn't be too cross with others, since she found it difficult to stop referring to herself as a girl. Perhaps that was a consequence of feeling no different than she had felt before the milestone. But was she resisting the natural pull of adulthood or the opposite, being much too old before her time? Her grandmother said Elise was born with an old soul, but Elise knew otherwise.

Carousel Boy's ability to pique her interest surprised her. She couldn't recall the last time she allowed herself to consider the possibility of romance, even intimacy. Of course there was the physical attraction—he was tall, trim, blond, focused, and good with children. He had an intensity that revealed itself in his piercing eyes. A neutral, unflappable expression and stiffness in movement out of character with his youthfulness gave him an air of mystery, as did the green canvas rucksack that he was never without. The adorable but reticent boy, she surmised, was either a very diligent worker or a serial killer.

"Shit! You're being too dramatic," Elise muttered aloud as her wrist pushed the kitchen faucet handle to stream even hotter water.

Her mind flickered with images of her obsession. Carousel Boy looked like a detached, impassive child, a contrast to the grinning imps and adolescents who climbed aboard the merry-go-round and waved to photo-snapping parents with each circled pass. *Carousel Boy wouldn't have fun on his own merry-go-round*. He wouldn't have been the squealing puppy of a boy who squirmed off the ride nor the pouty type who showed apprehension with tears. No, Carousel Boy was probably the child who sat quietly wherever his parents randomly placed him. An exercise in endurance, he'd neither return the adoring gazes of his mum or dad nor show the slightest interest in the ride's other exotic animals or their yelping riders. *Another wounded soul, perhaps? But huggable, yes, very huggable.*

Elise's thoughts focused on Carousel Boy's eyes. They were light—green, gray, maybe even blue. She'd have to get closer to know for sure. But the crinkles were unmistakable—and appealing. They gave him character, an air of kindness, even vulnerability, as did the slight hitch in his step that became more pronounced toward the end of an evening, a product of the crisp night air or, perhaps, only a sign of fatigue.

Shaking her wet hands over the sink, Elise nodded; a plan stirred in her head. Its boldness surprised her. "But yes! That's precisely what I'll do."

"Why don't you come by for a drink?"

Carousel Boy kept walking toward the merry-go-round. After a few paces, he slowed then stopped. His turn was cautious, almost timid. He removed the rucksack from his back and held it in front of him. He stared at Elise for a few seconds as if trying to determine whether the invitation had, in fact, been intended for him.

"Yes, you, Carousel Boy," Elise said with a smile and a nod toward the corner restaurant. "We serve good wine, champagne. Market vendors get a Christmas discount." She made that part up, but it didn't matter. She'd comp his drink for a chance to talk to him—to satisfy her curiosity.

She couldn't tell whether his pink cheeks meant that he blushed or responded to the nippy air in the same manner her fingers reacted to ice. He took a single step forward, stopped, then retreated to his initial footing. "I don't drink wine, especially the fizzy stuff."

Her arm swept backward toward the bar. "We've got beer too, plenty of it."

"I...I don't know," he stammered. "I shouldn't...not while I'm working."

So, Carousel Boy has morals. Many a Brussels laborer went about his workday sipping from cans of Jupiler and Maes.

Elise and Carousel Boy stared at each other in silence for a few more awkward seconds. Elise didn't know what to do. Complimenting his work ethic would sound patronizing. And she didn't want to beg, make herself sound desperate. Perhaps she simply needed more practice. *At least I tried.*

Elise shrugged. "Oh well, let's—"

"Parents don't like it so much," he said, talking over her, "when a guy with beer breath drives their little darlings, even if it's a two-minute ride on a merry-go-round."

Elise detected a faint movement at the corners of his mouth. *Is that how he smiles?* His crinkled eyes flashed with the hint of a sparkle. *Green. His eyes are green—the very same shade of his knapsack.*

She clapped her palms together, as much for satisfaction as for warmth. "After shift, then."

"Or maybe you want to ride the carousel." He studied her reaction, his chin down, tentative eyes peering from beneath his lowered brow. "I give a vendor discount too."

Elise let out a burst of laughter. "In that case, I call dibs on the winged unicorn. By the way, what's your name? Can't keep calling you Carousel Boy, can I?"

His lips parted to form the faintest of smiles. "Can if you want to, but it's Robbe. Robbe Wouters."

After that first conversation with Robbe, Elise waited for him to show up at her bar. She was sure he would. But days passed. She watched him come and go from his shift at the carousel. If their eyes happened to meet, he'd nod and even smile, but nothing more. She had a new plan.

During her dinner break, Elise made her way to the carousel. She got in line behind a tall couple, a man with a boy hoisted on his shoulders and a woman wearing a fluffy fur hat, gripping a little girl whose squeals and sobs signaled her misgivings for the ride.

At the head of the line, Elise assumed the voice of a little girl. She called out to a distracted Robbe, "Single ticket for the winged unicorn."

"Sorry, little girl. Animals are first come, first...*You*, it's *you*." A flustered Robbe took Elise by the hand and helped her mount the pink unicorn.

After an extended ride, Elise extracted Robbe's pledge to stop by for a drink at the end of the night. She wasn't sure he'd keep his promise. But her handsome Carousel Boy did come, green canvas backpack and all, as the seafood bar began to slow down after an exceptionally busy night.

"What took you so long?" Elise asked, yelling over the counter where patrons placed orders.

Robbe shrugged, nodding back to the giant lobster and crab that sat motionless on the darkened carousel. "Closest I ever get to shellfish. Can't stomach the stuff."

They both laughed, breaking the anxiety of the moment. After pouring two drinks, Elise pulled off her serving apron and stepped around the counter. Robbe stood somewhat awkwardly, one hand clutching the rucksack, the other tucked in his pocket. His face wore an almost frightened look. After handing him a dark beer, she clinked his glass with her champagne flute and led him to an empty high table.

"Anything else you care to share?"

"Huh?"

"Likes, dislikes, that kinda stuff. For example, you hate seafood. That's the first and only bit of information I know about you…besides your name, that is."

"W…well…I…uh…"

She patted his hand, which he withdrew. "Relax. I invited you for a beer, not an interrogation. Maybe we should just enjoy the drink. Not get too personal."

After a gulp from the tall glass, Robbe calmed. His breathing quieted. "No, it's okay. We're practically neighbors, work neighbors anyway."

"Then I should go first. It's only right since I—"

He rejected her proposal with a firm shake of his head. After taking another generous swig of beer he launched into his narrative. "Spoiled fish made me sick once. Threw up for days. Hate heights too. Fell as a boy…in Ieper, where I was born. Hurt my leg, almost broke my neck. That's all I hate, all I can remember anyway. Moved to Brussels five years ago after…" His gaze fell to the table before he regained his focus. "I'm twenty-three, by the way. Share a flat with three other guys in Forest—not the nice part, of course. And I love chicken, in case you were wondering what it was I ate." After a third gulp of beer he looked into her eyes, a look of satisfaction on his face.

Elise nodded. "Good start. Don't think I could handle too much more on my first glass of champagne." Elise began to formulate what she planned to share of her own history when she remembered something. "Oh, there is one more thing. That rucksack. Seems rather mysterious. Whatever are you hiding in there?"

Robbe pulled the bag toward him, clutching it to his chest. "Stuff, just stuff."

Elise dropped the subject. Curiosity had to take a backseat to budding romance. However, Robbe remained sullen as she launched into her history, his expression impassive even after she confided a long estrangement from her family. She shared the news she had received from a former neighbor of her parents. Her mother and stepfather had recently relocated from Brussels to a small village in the Wallonian countryside. "Guess that means I'm not invited for Christmas," she added with a forced laugh.

The conversation never regained its initial momentum. When Robbe turned down the offer of a refill and bid her a curt goodbye, Elise figured that was the end of her brief flirtation—not much longer than a ride on the carousel, but infinitely better than a case of lousy Canadian chocolate. Quaffing a second glass of champagne, Elise watched Robbe retreat into the night, his backpack slung over one shoulder.

But to Elise's surprise, Robbe showed up after shift the very next night and the night after that. He adopted a greeting of encasing her icy fingers in his large, strong palms until the warmth returned. Her fondness for him grew, yet she knew enough not to ask too many personal questions—the backpack was off-limits. Still, she learned that they had some things in common: neither had siblings, their fathers were dead, and both hated school and liked blues music, science-fiction movies, and *pommes frites* drowning in mayonnaise. Over the next couple of weeks, things progressed. In fact, Robbe and Elise were going on their first official date three days before Christmas.

Elise stood at the kitchen sink, her hands under the hot water. She was a jumble of nervous energy, a mix of exhilaration and dread. She didn't remember who had invited whom. She wanted to believe the date set for the following evening, their first rendezvous outside Place Sainte-Catherine, was Robbe's idea, but it was probably hers.

Her gaze wandered out the window, over the line of empty wine bottles, their mouths seasonally stuffed with green and red tapers. In spite of the coal-black sky of the winter solstice, Elise thought the night bright and joyous. The neighborhood was at its peak of seasonal cheer. Colorful light strings flickered through the veiled mist. Vibrant pops of orange, red, blue, green, and white multiplied, refracted through millions of drizzle specks. A veritable forest of Christmas trees glowed in windows and on balconies. Her spirit soared as if taking flight on one of the merry-go-round's fantastic winged creatures.

Satisfied that warmth had returned to her fingers, Elise shut off the kitchen faucet and lit the holiday candles. In the living room, she flicked on the lights of a small Christmas tree, her first since moving to Brussels—actually, her first since her father had died. Her thoughts turned to Robbe and what she'd wear the following night.

The modern bar Elise suggested, located just outside the Galeries Saint-Hubert, was neutral ground. Packed with locals, expats, and tourists, the popular night spot offered plenty of diversions should the pressures of a "first date" stifle the conversation.

Dressed in a short gray wool skirt and red sweater purchased that afternoon from H&M, Elise walked into the dimly lit bar. Her stomach bubbled with nerves. She scanned the room before spotting Robbe. She couldn't say for sure, but it looked as if he had a new haircut in addition to a fresh shave. As she approached, she noted that his button-down collared shirt still had the packaging creases. And although the trousers were washed, they were the same dark khakis he rotated into his shifts at the carousel. But the cologne, a musky scent of earthy spices that reminded her of a forest, was new. She hadn't considered Robbe the cologne type.

He stood when she approached the table, grabbing and rubbing her hands out of habit. She let him, though her fingers weren't the least bit chilled.

She kissed his cheek in greeting. "Hope you didn't mind my suggesting this place?" A rendezvous at her flat would have required heavy cleaning and apologies for her shabby neighborhood—and quite possibly some expectations, especially at the end of the night. She wasn't ready for that, not on her first real date in years.

"Course not, location's perfect for both of—"

"It's just that I…Oh, oh, so sorry. I just talked over—"

The server's arrival interrupted Elise's nervous apology. They ordered drinks and a plate of assorted cheeses. She assumed first-date jitters were the cause of Robbe's fidgeting although, perhaps, he just needed to use the toilet. For that purpose, he promptly excused himself.

Elise used his absence to check her makeup and collect her thoughts. She hadn't yet decided how much more of her past she wanted to share. Did he need to know that this was her first date in six years, that she'd finally mustered the confidence and courage to risk opening her heart to another human being? If the conversation drifted in that direction, could she tell him why? *Hell! Stop overanalyzing. Have fun.* She returned her lipstick to her purse. She hadn't noticed it at first; she'd almost forgotten about it. But there on the bench next to Robbe's seat sat the green canvas backpack.

She struggled with her conscience. What if Robbe suddenly returned? She was violating his trust. But if she were quick, he'd never know. She'd satisfy her curiosity and macabre sense of humor. *My luck, I'll find a severed head!*

With her eyes on the staircase that led up to the toilets, she leaned over the table. Her hands were on the bag. Her fingers traced the zipper to the tab. She could feel her heart race. She cringed at the zipping sound. She felt a presence behind her. She froze. Possible excuses clicked through her mind—each feeble, unbelievable. She turned to face the consequences.

"Cosmo for you," said the server, placing a glass before her, "and beer for the gentleman."

After taking a large sip of her drink, Elise couldn't help but laugh at herself. Though her conscience stirred with guilt, she'd come that far. Besides, the bag was already open. Perhaps the alcohol gave her courage. The first thing she found was a gift-wrapped box.

A present—for me?

She cringed. She'd not gotten Robbe anything. A gift exchange was, she reasoned, too intimate, too presumptuous. Shaking off the distraction, Elise returned to her mission. Besides a wool hat, scarf, and gloves, her hand felt something unexpected: the soft, matted fur of a child's plaything. Opening the bag further, she peered inside and saw a black and white stuffed animal. Though worn and tattered, it was unmistakably a toy kitten.

Elise didn't have time to think. She recognized Robbe's legs on the stairs leading from the toilet. She had just enough time to repack the contents and zip the bag back up.

Even though the evening was a success by all accounts, with only a few awkward silences, Elise couldn't shake the image of the stuffed kitten. *Whatever does it mean?*

A few months later, Elise finally had an incentive for giving her flat the heavy cleaning it needed. Robbe had accepted her invitation for a home-cooked meal. She didn't know if the evening would progress to sex. But she was prepared if it did. She'd been in no hurry to push their relationship to that level. And neither, it seemed, had Robbe. She appreciated the slow and deliberate pace at which they took things, an old-fashioned romance. Establishing a foundation of trust was important to her as was growing her confidence. After spending most weekends and several weekday evenings together for nearly four months, sexual intimacy was the next logical step. If Robbe didn't bring up the subject, Elise intended to take matters into her own hands.

After lighting the candles on the table, and setting her phone's music library on shuffle, Elise checked herself in the mirror. She clutched the simple amber pendant that dangled from a chain around her neck. The ancient creature encased inside the yellow resin was a source of wonder to her. *The insect didn't have the strength to escape its fate. Yet, that moment of weakness preserved it forever.* She pondered whether that was a fair or tragic trade-off.

The pendant had been Robbe's Christmas present, the gift inside the wrapped box she had discovered in his rucksack that night at the bar. When she apologized for not getting him anything, he was so sweet. He insisted the amber piece was nothing extravagant, merely a little something bought at cost from a Polish merchant at the Christmas market. But Elise knew better and, whatever the value, she thought it the most beautiful pendant in the world, the first and only piece of jewelry anyone ever gave her.

"Great meal," Robbe said as Elise cleared the table of roasted chicken and vegetables. "Most nights I just grab something from the market." After Christmas, when the carousel moved on to provincial fairs and festivals, Robbe returned to his regular job. He worked for a Flemish outfit that sold fruits and vegetables at various daily markets throughout Brussels.

"More wine?"

Robbe nodded his acceptance. Elise was pleased that his tastes grew beyond simply beer. After filling both glasses, she suggested they move to the sofa.

Lowering the music volume, Elise sat beside him. Taking a deep breath, she clasped his hand in hers. "I like you, Robbe. And, I think you…you like me too."

"A lot. I like you a lot." After placing his wineglass on the coffee table, he kissed her on the cheek.

She looked into his eyes. "You know you're the first boy…er, guy I've dated in years."

"Uh-huh."

"But I never told you why."

"Don't have to. Not necessary."

Elise sensed his anxiety level rising. Was he afraid of what she'd say or how he'd react? "It is necessary. And important to me…important for us, for our relationship."

He grew fidgety; his face turned pale. "Why do we have to mess with things?"

"To grow, Robbe. To move to…We've been…*exclusive*…for almost four months. I'd like to…to take our relationship to the next step. That is, if you want to?"

"Course I want to." His expression was as tentative as his tone.

"Before we do, I've got things I want—no, *need*—to tell you." Elise had decided that Robbe deserved to know what he was getting into before he invested too much. He was fragile; she didn't want to break him with deception. And if she were honest with herself, perhaps she wanted to test the depth of his commitment. She'd waited a long time for this moment—perhaps she was still a little fragile too.

Robbe sighed; a look of surrender swept across his face.

Elise took a swig of wine. She'd rehearsed her words for days. "I've told you that I was thirteen when my mother remarried. I didn't tell you she did it for security, not love. I don't think she even liked…him." Even then, Elise couldn't bring herself to utter her stepfather's name.

"The abuse began shortly after my mother's new husband moved in with us. It started slowly…caresses, light groping. I wasn't sure what was happening. Soon, he needed more…to be satisfied. Then it hurt… it hurt bad. I was scared, ashamed."

Elise studied Robbe's face. Shock gave way to sadness and compassion. He hurt for her, but she needed to continue to get it all out. She clutched his hand.

"He twisted things. Made me feel dirty, as if I were to blame." Her stepfather made it seem as if the abuse wasn't something he did *to* her, but rather a consensual act of pleasure *they* shared. "I couldn't tell my mother." Her mother was weak, a victim of her new husband's emotional abuse. "I didn't think she'd believe me…or even *want* to believe me." Elise endured the abuse for three years before mustering the courage to stop things. She found her inspiration in books with strong, brave girls and young women. "If they could find the strength to fight back and triumph, why couldn't I?"

At sixteen, Elise informed her mother that she planned to confront her stepfather with or without her approval. Her mother locked herself in her bedroom. "I could hear the sobs through the door. Didn't take her long to transfer the hurt and betrayal she felt for him into anger toward *me*. Of course, at the time, I didn't understand why she was so furious with me."

"I'm so sorry, Elise, so very sorry."

Caressing Robbe's cheek, Elise described the confrontation with her stepfather. "He stood there and laughed…laughed as if it were a joke. As if *I* were a joke." Elise had already made up her mind to leave home. She moved in with her grandmother and lived there until the old woman died. "Got counseling. Didn't take to it at first. Thought it helped me label things, but not much more. Stuck with it though—had enough sense to do that. What my stepfather did changed me…forever. I needed help finding my way forward." Elise took a deep breath. She squeezed Robbe's hand. "Made up my mind I wasn't going to let it define me, cripple me. I felt liberated. But I couldn't put it behind me…not completely. Not sure something like that can ever be forgotten."

Robbe pressed her hand to his lips. "My dear, sweet Elise. You poor girl." He pulled her head to his chest and kissed the top of her head, repeating "sorry" in a whisper, his voice choked with tears.

Sitting up, Elise looked into his eyes. "I survived, Robbe. I'm alive, happy. I'm strong, very strong. I like that most of all. I want the same… for you."

Robbe stared at her, his expression turning from sympathy to shock. "For *me?*"

Elise was nearly as shocked. Where did her words come from? Why had she said that about Robbe? Perhaps opening up about her past stoked suspicions based on long-dormant memories. Maybe she finally recognized in Robbe's soulful eyes and sudden bouts of sullenness what she once saw in herself. Had she and Robbe gravitated toward each other because they shared a common history? Had they felt the pull of kindred spirits?

Visibly shaken, Robbe got up. Stammering something about feeling ill, he grabbed his coat. He paused at the door and turned. "I'm sorry, so sorry."

Elise ran to the door, but he was gone. She didn't hear from him the next day. Her calls to him went unanswered. She visited the daily markets where he worked, but his co-workers hadn't seen him. His roommates hadn't seen him either.

Two weeks later, Elise's eyes lit up when she looked at the display on her phone. Robbe's text offered an apology. He hoped she could forgive him. He wanted to meet to explain. He suggested a coffee shop on Rue de Midi.

Although Robbe greeted her with a hug and kiss, he seemed different—distracted, distant. He apologized again for disappearing, and shook off questions of his well-being with a terse "Fine, I'm fine."

His glazed eyes, blank expression, and disheveled appearance suggested otherwise.

As they sat sipping coffee, Elise took his hand. "I'm not angry. Concerned, that's all. I care about you, Robbe."

"And I you." He sighed. "Oh, Elise, you were incredibly brave to tell me about your…your stepfather. And strong, so very strong to stop things. That's why…why I wanted to see you. To explain. To tell you…" Rising emotions choked Robbe's words. Elise caressed his cheek until he calmed. "I need to tell you the kind of person I am."

"Robbe, I don't—"

He pulsed his steepled hands against his quivering lips. "Please… let me talk. This isn't easy for me."

Robbe leaned over the table, his stammering voice dropping to a whisper. "After my father died, Mother grew depressed. I don't think I've ever seen anyone so sad." His mother's sullen mood, he explained, lifted during their playful sessions of kissing and hugging. He liked making her happy. But the teasing soon escalated. Like Elise, Robbe didn't know it was abuse—at first. After he began to feel uneasy, anxious, and scared, his mother gave him a stuffed kitten to quiet his sobs. "Maybe it was a bribe, a pacifier. I see that now. But it smelled of her perfume. Reminded me of my mother, of her love."

Elise shuddered. She understood the significance of the stuffed kitten, why he couldn't let it go. Although it pained her to hear Robbe's ordeal, she owed it to him to listen. He'd done the same for her. She cradled the amber pendant at her throat. Her silent nod signaled him to continue.

Pressing his hand to his cheek, Robbe took a deep breath. Elise sensed his inner turmoil. She ached for him. "One night," he began, "she…she did things she hadn't done before." He paused. With a mix of determination and fear in his expression, Robbe stared at Elise. She understood what he wanted. She nodded her acknowledgment of the dark secret he had just revealed. "I bolted from her bed," he continued. "She stood in front of the door trying to calm me, telling me it was okay."

The urge to escape was so strong he didn't consider the consequences. "I turned. Pushed open the window, and jumped." His leg fractured in multiple places; he almost broke his neck. His mother was hysterical, screaming to the ambulance drivers and doctors to save her little man. "I heard her at my bedside when she thought I was asleep. She swore to God she'd never lay a hand on her little boy again if He saved me."

His mother kept her promise. But her pain didn't disappear. She turned to alcohol and painkillers. "As she sobbed in the dark, I lay in bed clinging to my kitten." He clung to his mother's love, clung to the past. He asked God to let them go back to being a happy family again.

"I killed her."

"Robbe, no! You—"

He took Elise's hand from his cheek and pressed it gently to the table. "B...but even worse..." He began to quake, holding back tears. "The vodka and pills were killing her. I saw her slipping away from me."

"My poor Robbe. I'm—"

Again, he deflected her offered hand. "Elise, I...I...told her she could...do things to me...like she did before." He closed his eyes; despair reflected in his face. "I'm a bad, horrible person!"

"Oh, my dear, sweet Robbe. You're not bad or horrible. You're...an angel."

Rather than comforting him, the word electrified Robbe. He stiffened, his voice rising with passion. "I was willing to let my own mother abuse me, Elise." Robbe covered his eyes. He shook with tears.

Elise squeezed his arm and caressed the top of his head. "Listen to me. Something inside you told you it was wrong. That's why you jumped. You were a brave little boy. What your mother did to you was wrong. She realized that...paid for her sins." Elise knew that his mother died from liver failure five years ago. "There's been enough suffering," she added. "You're a good, decent man."

Robbe lowered his hands from his face. She recognized in his dull green eyes the same mix of sadness, fear, anger, and disgust that had stared back at her in the mirror during the height of her stepfather's abuse, the same mix of toxic rage and self-loathing that took her years of therapy to tame.

She clutched his hands. "Let me help you."

"I need time. Need to figure things out."

Extracting his hands, Robbe rose from the café chair and walked toward the door. Elise waited, expecting him to stop, to turn, say goodbye. Instead he walked out without looking back. He disappeared into the crowded street.

For months Elise replayed the scene. Why didn't she try to stop him, run after him? Perhaps she wasn't ready for a relationship after all. Maybe she'd failed *his* test. She hated herself for what she should have done, but didn't, what she should have said, but couldn't. She had stared at his empty chair in the café and spoke the words that came too late, "I love you, Robbe Wouters." But he was gone.

A spike in workers, the sound of hammers, and the noticeable nip in the air informed Elise that Place Sainte-Catherine and the surrounding streets would soon welcome the annual Christmas market. Not really interested in the food and ware stalls, she watched with anticipation as workers readied the fantastical carousel. But the ride's whimsical creatures were no longer a source of wonder. Only one question consumed her. Would Robbe return to the carousel?

She hadn't seen nor heard from Robbe since that afternoon in the coffee shop months before. When the Christmas market finally opened to the public, Elise wasn't surprised by the appearance of a new carousel boy. But she was surprised by her reaction. Every glance at the carousel without Robbe filled her with immense grief, the sense of loss, a feeling of wasted opportunity and lost love. Her fingers never felt so cold, so raw. Her heart ached with the same chill.

For weeks, the funk that enveloped Elise never released its grip. The Christmas market lost its magic. Holiday mirth was hollow. The longest night of the year arrived. Unlike the prior year, it held no joy for Elise. With a forlorn glance at the carousel, she bent over the stainless-steel trough to retrieve another bottle of champagne for a rowdy table of stockbroker dandies.

"Interested in a ride on the winged unicorn?"

Elise took a few seconds to process the voice. With her heart beginning to race, she looked up from the trough. There stood Robbe, hair cut, freshly shaven, and smelling like the forest floor. He waved two carousel tickets in the air. Elise sensed that something was different, out of place. *The green rucksack.* Robbe no longer carried the backpack. His green eyes sparkled and the smile was genuine. Some of the former sorrow and confusion remained in his expression, but it seemed tempered, less pronounced. She recalled her own long journey of recovery. *He's getting better*, she thought. *My Robbe's working through things.*

Elise felt tears welling in her eyes as she ran around the counter. Before she could wrap her arms around his neck, Robbe grabbed her hands. He pressed them between his warm palms to erase the chill. Laughing and crying at the same time, Elise kissed her Carousel Boy. When he released her hands, she squeezed him tight. This time, she'd never let go.

Recycled Promises

"Sell, keep, toss, give away." Samantha Thomas stooped over a box in the dining room of her townhouse. Her husband Nick tracked her sorting decisions with a series of self-adhesive notes. He tagged those items they hoped to sell with a pink square. Things intended for the journey back to the States got a yellow square. Blue meant the trash heap, and green, give away.

"What about your laurel tree?"

Samantha stood up and smoothed her long blonde hair. She looked to the back of the apartment where a lush walled garden was visible through tall French doors. "Forgot about that. All my potted plants, really."

"Food and liquor too, and spices. Can't take any of that back. Them's the rules."

"Green sticker, Nicky. We'll give all that away. Annie next door might want some of those things, especially the alcohol. She and Tim are quite the drinkers."

Nick glanced at her with raised eyebrows before adding, "Did we have this much work on the way over here?"

Samantha ran her hand down her husband's flannel sleeve and laughed. "One of us did. The other buried himself in work. Remember?"

Nick kissed her cheek. "Believe me, Sam. I know I couldn't have done this without you."

Nick and Samantha Thomas had moved to Brussels from

Detroit three years earlier. An engineer by profession, Nick pleaded with his boss to send him to Belgium to keep an eye on a company subsidiary, a small manufacturer that made train instruments and other components for the transportation industry. The assignment's open-ended term bothered Nick and Samantha's families more than it did the childfree couple. Along with their careers, travel had always provided a satisfactory substitute for children.

The couple looked at the posting as a great adventure and, more importantly, a fresh start, not only for Nick's career but also for their marriage. A Brussels base afforded them the chance to visit cities like Paris and London. In addition, their central location facilitated the exploration of the quaint villages and rural landscapes of Germany, France, and Italy that most Americans skipped on their grand tours of Europe.

Sam sighed. "Been a great adventure. Guess I thought we might stay."

Nick put his arm around Sam and pulled her toward him. "Me too, honey. I'm sorry."

"Nicky dear, don't be sorry. How could you know they'd send you back so soon? No, your goal was to bring us to Europe. On that, you succeeded. I'm just saying…you know…in a way, we've only just settled in."

"Thanks to you. You did an amazing job of turning this old house into a home. Garden's a masterpiece. Our social circle was entirely your doing. What would we have done without your garden and expat clubs?" He nuzzled her neck; she leaned away.

Sam wasn't conscious of withdrawing from Nick's affection until she saw the look of surprise on her husband's face. *Why'd I do that*? she asked herself. But Nick didn't say anything so she let the awkward moment pass without comment, dismissing her reaction as mere stress of the move.

Sam sat back down on the thick wool rug and crossed her legs. Digging into a box, she plucked out a magazine and studied its cover.

The lower corner highlighted current articles including a monthly feature, "Get to Know the Expats." Sam saved the issue because she was featured in an article entitled "Samantha Thomas: Novice Gardener Finds Fertile Ground in Brussels." She didn't know how *Expat Life* had obtained her contact information, but its request for an interview flattered her. She'd never been the subject of a magazine article. In addition, at the time of the interview, she was feeling particularly vulnerable, low-spirited. The transition from successful corporate manager with a paycheck and a purpose of her own to life as a stay-at-home spouse of an expat wasn't easy.

She waved the magazine in the air. "Remember this, Nicky? My one claim to fame."

An odd expression flashed across her husband's face. But the mix of surprise and shock quickly faded. He kissed the top of her head. "One of many, honey, one of many."

Sam flipped through the pages until she came to the full-page photo of Nick and her. She'd sent the interviewer, a kind but overly inquisitive woman named Natalie Chamblis, a few digital pictures to enhance the article. Sam was pleased that Natalie chose for the full page the selfie that Nick had snapped of the couple in their new garden. They looked happy. Nick had just gotten his first haircut in Brussels, his thick dark hair shorter than usual. The navy-blue polo shirt he wore brought out the softness of his baby-blue eyes. His free arm draped around Sam's shoulder. Her pink and white sweatshirt played off the deep red rhododendron she had just finished planting.

Staring at the magazine photo, Sam recalled the great sense of accomplishment she felt at that exact moment. She didn't even mind the dirt smudges on her pullover or the oversized garden gloves. Natalie said those things gave the picture authenticity. Sam studied her grin; it made her look sincere, confident—strong. She especially liked the way Nick's gaze focused more on her than the camera. She detected true affection in that glance. She needed to feel his love at that moment, probably more than ever before in their fifteen-year marriage.

The article began on the facing page:

Putting Down New Roots

Samantha and Nick Thomas gave up suburban Detroit and said goodbye to friends and family for a fresh adventure in Belgium. Like most expats, they found the first several weeks of their new life exciting—and busy. The couple set up house in central Brussels. Outside, a vibrant city dazzled the uprooted transplants as if they were wide-eyed tourists. But then what? With Nick's demanding job and travel schedule that take him across Europe, how does Samantha fill her days?

How to fill her time was only one question Samantha faced during those gloomy days of early spring. She thought the drizzle would never stop. She and Nick had been in Brussels for what, two, three months? Nick was gone all the time, working late when he was in town or traveling to who knew where. It was silly of her to suspect he was having an affair. What happened in Detroit was an isolated digression, the very reason he lobbied so hard for the expat assignment, as a matter of fact—the fresh start, a chance to rebuild their marriage without distractions of the past. No, logic told her that her husband was trying to prove himself, show his employer that he was worth the investment of moving him to Europe. Sam hated being angry with Nick. He had enough stress without her unloading on him. Instead, she kept her frustrations and sadness bottled inside.

If it were possible, she would have willed herself invisible. In a way, that was how she felt. The Belgium resident card for Nick was relatively easy to obtain. Sam, on the other hand, had to make several trips to meet with the stone faces at Town Hall before they found her in the system. Even then, it took half a dozen attempts for their digital machine to register her fingerprints. Maybe she was invisible.

Nick's new Belgian colleagues didn't ease her transition either. In

Detroit, Nick and Sam had made a point of reaching out to fellow workers new to the city. Perhaps that was why she had anticipated the same hospitality in Brussels. But even Nick's boss, a well-connected local, made no effort to help the couple adjust to their new surroundings. No, Sam was invisible to Advanced Technologies as well.

And then there were the issues with a bank account and credit card. The exotic-looking woman at the bank fawned over Nick. But with no income of her own anymore, Sam couldn't get the bank to issue her a credit card. And in a surrealistic twist of irony, the bank required Sam to sign a document allowing the bank to seize her assets should Nick default on his account. Maybe it didn't matter. Every bill was in Nick's name anyway. At some point during those early weeks in Brussels, an exasperated Sam slid the post office box key from her key ring and slammed it onto the kitchen counter. "Here," she said to Nick. "Take it. All the mail's in your name anyway."

As for a car, Sam couldn't drive the company-issued BMW. The vehicle was registered solely in Nick's name. Besides, Sam had never learned to drive a standard shift. The narrow streets and poor driving skills of the Belgians gave her no incentive to learn. In the eyes of their bank, their landlord, utility companies, city officials, and Nick's unsociable colleagues, Samantha Thomas didn't exist. With no friends or social life, and an absentee husband, she felt like a nobody.

Sam had experienced depression before, short bouts that usually began with a major disappointment or a series of minor frustrations that clustered into something bigger. But she had always navigated across those narrow channels with little effort, never losing sight of either shore. In Detroit, Sam could turn to her job and family for purpose, comfort, and fulfillment. A challenging new project at work or a shopping spree and spa day with her mother and sisters usually bumped her from her funks.

Even Nick's brief affair with a co-worker in Detroit had filled her more with anger and sadness than with classic depression. Perhaps her husband's fling didn't last long enough and his remorse was so profound and sincere to stir deeper emotions. There was, of course, the daunting task of the Brussels move that left little time for self-reflection and pity.

However, what Sam began to experience in Brussels was bigger, scarier. Episodes were more ominous than anything she'd ever before endured. A shadow descended upon her. Surrounded by some great, immeasurable creature, Sam felt helpless. Most times, all she could do was lie on the bed and hope the dark spell would pass. She never understood what caused the beast to finally release her from its sticky tentacles. There was no visible cause and effect, nothing to learn and apply to the next bout. She emerged from the gloom as if drifting on a languid current toward shore. She grew to fear those episodes. They took her to unfamiliar places, darker than she'd ever known.

What was it that Carl Sandburg wrote? *The fog comes on little cat feet.* That slow, stalking movement is how Sam came to think of depression's onset. She sensed its approach but was helpless to thwart its advance. It crept ever closer, finally pouncing, ensnaring some stray thought or idea. Once in its clutches, she was engulfed in numbness. She grew weak, lethargic. Her spirit succumbed as if the beast had injected her with a paralyzing poison, keeping her barely conscious like a fly caught in the clutches of an exotic plant or a spider web. She was a hapless victim fighting to live until the exhaustion of escape was more daunting than surrender.

Trapped in that gripping cycle of depression, Sam became confounded. Did she grow to accept, even welcome, the dark moods? They became familiar. And in her new world that was so foreign and unwelcoming, familiarity didn't so much breed contempt as provide comfort. "Might someone," she asked herself, "become addicted to depression as they would painkillers and alcohol?" Was depression her addiction? "No!" she told herself. "I don't enjoy the mind-numbing bouts." She merely greeted them as one might an old acquaintance whose company isn't so much enjoyed as endured. An alternative to expending energy on discovery, the descent into depression became as easy as treading a well-worn path—the difference between hacking through a jungle and tumbling down a polished slide.

The interview and magazine article, therefore, had been a well-timed lifeline. Sam needed the boost of confidence. Even though she was never more than a voice on the phone, Natalie gave her someone to talk to, and, more importantly, a kindred spirit, a sympathetic ear to which she could freely vent. Natalie, also the wife of an expat, struggled with loneliness too. Her own lifeline, she confessed, had been the freelance job with the magazine. Natalie suggested expat organizations as a cure for Sam's loneliness.

Sam's depression eased after she took Natalie's advice. Exploring the Internet, she found Green Thumbs, a mix of expats, male and female, who shared a love of gardening. Although a novice, Sam desired to learn more. She had a huge, untended garden at the back of their apartment as a blank slate. The Green Thumbs steered her toward the best annuals and soils for use in the cool, wet Belgian summers. The first year, before she was privy to the club's sage advice, Sam's geraniums, petunias, and impatiens drowned after a rainy spell that lasted weeks.

Sam also joined a second organization, Expat Voyagers, run by a Dutchman who arranged day trips for expats. The well-planned coach tours took groups to places of interest such as Holland's Keukenhof Garden for spring tulips, Cologne and Dusseldorf for Christmas markets, France's Champagne region, and Germany's Mosel River Valley for wine. Even when Nick bowed out due to heavy workloads, the tours brought camaraderie and pleasure to a lonely Sam. On one such occasion, Sam offered Nick's unused ticket to their neighbor Annie. As a result, their friendship blossomed. Annie's husband Tim, a diplomat with the European Union, was away from home more often than Nick. Annie sought in drink, relief from her loneliness and suspicions of her husband's infidelity.

The Green Thumbs and Expat Voyagers provided social outlet. The latter group's organized coffee meet-ups allowed Sam to have conversations with interesting people. Although she dismissed the flirtations from one handsome expat spouse as harmless, she was nonetheless flattered. Her insecurities and feeling of invisibility faded.

She and Nick began to throw parties similar to the ones they had hosted in Detroit. Their new friends provided dates for dinners and other social functions. These were expats from all over the world whose commonality consisted chiefly of a capacity for speaking English and a shared understanding of the travails of navigating Belgium's unique quirks and annoyances. It was nice to have friends with whom to commiserate about the need for a down jacket during summer, disruptions due to frequent strikes, the lack of Mexican food, and the slow, frustrating government bureaucracy. Being half of a sociable couple was one of the things that Sam enjoyed most. Brussels started to feel more like home.

"All the electronics have to go."

"Huh?" Sam closed the magazine and placed it on the "keep" pile.

"The electronics. Gotta try to sell them all."

"I still don't understand why the world can't agree on a standardized current."

"We'll probably take a bath on the treadmill. May just have to give it away."

"Well worth it anyway. You've never been in better shape," Samantha said, reaching for her coffee. She paused to consider the memories represented by the porcelain mug.

The couple started collecting the bright mugs from an international coffee chain to fill a basic need. They had sold or donated most of their household goods in Detroit. As the souvenir mugs began to fill their kitchen shelves, Sam viewed them as a way to record their travels with something more useful than a dust-catching knickknack. Her morning trips to the cupboard sparked memories of lovely weekends with Nick in Copenhagen, Lisbon, Stockholm, and Paris among other places.

She didn't have the same attachment for the mugs Nick brought back as souvenirs from his business trips to Barcelona, Oslo, and Prague. But Sam never mentioned anything—she didn't want to spoil *his* special memories.

"The mugs are all keepers," Sam said, hoisting the one in her hand. "Even Nice?"

Sam laughed. "Even Nice."

Nice had not been nice to the couple. Nick had been a real sweetheart, arranging the getaway for her fortieth birthday. But their visit to the south of France coincided with the fiercest storm to hit the area in years. They didn't see a single patch of blue sky or sea, only gray. Cold, horizontal rain drenched them raw. Someone even stole Nick's umbrella from a stand beside the door of a quaint restaurant in the old town. They scurried back to their hotel through the narrow cobblestone streets clutching each other like they did when they were first married. They laughed when Sam's umbrella blew inside out, soaking them both. Despite the inclement weather, that weekend marked a turning point. Sam felt they had finally put Detroit behind them.

Sam considered the blue mug in her hand and smiled. A bicycle perched on a bridge over one of the city's iconic canals recalled Amsterdam and another lovely weekend. "We've had quite the adventure."

Nick squeezed her shoulders. "There'll be more adventures ahead. Of that I'm sure."

She gazed up at his face. His strong dimpled chin, high cheekbones, and full lips made him as handsome as the day she first laid eyes on him. "You know, Nicky, I'm a bit scared about going home."

He sat down on the carpet and faced her. He reached for her hand. "Me too."

It wasn't the first time the couple discussed their apprehension at returning home. Their adventure had changed them in ways that they themselves probably didn't understand. Other friends who repatriated to the States had similar warnings. "Don't expect to fall back into your old routine," they warned. "It'll be hard. Friends and family haven't had the same journey. They haven't changed, but you have."

"It'll take some time to settle back into our former life."

"That's just it," Sam said. "I don't want to go back to our old life. Don't know what I want, but I know I don't want to slot right back in where I left off." Even Sam knew her apprehension about returning to their former life in the States sounded strange, especially after her rough start in Belgium and the dark days second-guessing the company's relocating them to Europe. But she'd grown and, more importantly, moved beyond their past.

"I understand, honey." Nick said as if guessing her concern. "I'm a new man. I promise."

Sam shook the thoughts from her head, chuckling as she held up correspondence from their local town hall. Brussels was composed of nineteen semi-autonomous municipalities known as communes. "Here, honey, what about this?"

Nick groaned. "Toss. No, *burn*."

A few weeks earlier, the couple had received notice of a pending fine imposed because of their improper disposal of garbage. Brussels' waste collection and recycling system had noble intentions but cumbersome rules. Glass had to be carted for blocks to unsightly receptacles. Small slots required placing items into the bin, one by one. Sam always felt embarrassed after a party when she stood for several minutes feeding dozens of liquor bottles into the receptacle. Nick laughed when she told him that she had learned to say *"grand fête,"* meaning "big party," when people happened upon her at the recycling stations. "I don't want anyone to think we're alcoholics," she said in her defense.

As for other trash, blue bags were for plastic, yellow for paper, green for yard waste, and white for general refuse. Refuse workers collected white and green bags every Wednesday; yellow and blue bags were collected on alternating weeks.

In issuing a fine, the Town Hall alleged that the couple offered a yellow bag on a blue-bag day. In addition, Town Hall officials asserted that city workers found the couple's yellow bag several streets away, an even more serious infraction for commune bureaucrats.

"Why on earth would we cart our trash over a mile from the house?" Nick said at the time Sam brought the original notice home. "How do they know it's our garbage anyway? Must be a scam."

Assuming an angry tone, Nick had demanded that she drop the matter. "Dealings with Town Hall are neither quick nor painless." But Sam appealed anyway. She was sure that if she hadn't made a rare visit to the post office box and collected the notice, Nick would have merely paid the fine and never mentioned anything.

While the couple geared up for the move home, Sam awaited the response to her strongly worded appeal. She hoped for a reduced fine. In researching the infraction, she was starting to think that Nick was right. It probably was a scam. Annie and Tim and others in their expat circle were hit with a similar hefty fine. All urged her to appeal. Most got the pending fines reduced to as little as twenty-five euros.

As Sam tossed the Town Hall's correspondence into the "toss" pile, she teased her husband with a smirk. "We'll see who gets the last laugh, Mr. Know-It-All. Won't you be embarrassed when they cut the fine from two hundred and fifty euros to twenty-five."

But would they get the response to Sam's appeal before they left Brussels?

Two weeks later, while movers invaded their apartment, Sam slipped the post office box key from Nick's key ring and headed for the post office. Her husband was too preoccupied with the packing supervisor to notice. She had a few final postcards to send to her mom and sisters, and figured she'd do one final sweep of the box before they left town.

Among the monthly bills addressed to Nick, Sam found a letter from the Town Hall. Sam was excited. Had she succeeded in her appeal put together in Internet-translated French? Would she, just as Annie next door, get a reduced fine of only twenty-five euros? She had told Nick that due to his staunch opposition to an appeal, any reduction from the original fine was hers as a bounty.

"It'll serve him right to fork over two hundred euros," she muttered to herself as she tore open the envelope.

She scanned the cover letter. Of course, it was in French. She saw an amount, "200 euros," and understood its meaning. She was disappointed that the adjusted fine wasn't more in line with the lower amounts given to her friends.

"At least it's something," Sam said aloud.

She couldn't wait to boast of her success to Nick. *Fifty euros is fifty euros.* He'd have to apologize. Sam flipped through the rest of the reply. *I don't understand.* Attached to the Town Hall's reply were pages containing photocopies of multiple envelopes, bills and personal correspondence addressed to Nick Thomas at the couple's post office box. The return address on several envelopes drew Sam's attention. She stared at the copies but couldn't make sense of them. Her brain felt disconnected from her eyes. The sender's name was, Natalie Chamblis, the woman from *Expat Life*. And not merely one—half a dozen sent over a one-month period. A sense of dread swept over Sam.

After stuffing the correspondence into her purse, Sam ran home. She needed to get to the computer—to decipher the whole letter. She copied the French text into the application. The English translation was instantaneous if not completely lucid.

Since it was the couple's first offense, Town Hall officials agreed to a reduced fine. However, they firmly denied Sam's claim that this was not the Thomas's garbage. As proof, the Town Hall enclosed copies of the couple's correspondence. If further proof was desired, additional evidence would be made available for review in the commune's offices. This evidence, they wrote, included holiday photos of the couple with handwritten notes on the back—"Barcelona," "Prague," and "Oslo."

Sam's eyes darted from the computer screen to the desktop and the actual correspondence. Her fingers rifled through the pages hoping that the Town Hall had made a mistake. Her gaze rested on another photocopy. Somehow in her rush at the post office she'd overlooked the document. Though it wasn't a color copy, she recognized Advanced Technologies' letterhead. Confusion surrendered to fury as she read: "Though reluctant to do so based on our sizable investment in moving you and your family to Brussels, we agree to your immediate relocation back to Detroit for personal reasons. It is our sincere hope that your wife's health improves quickly...."

After shoving the Town Hall's correspondence back into her purse, Sam's quivering fingers fumbled on the keyboard. *Damn computer!* She had to turn it off, blacken the screen, blot out the sickening facts that stared at her in black and white. She ran her fingers through her hair, pausing to tug at the roots, wishing she could pull the hornet's nest of dark thoughts and vile images from her mind. *Lies. All lies.* She started to rise but collapsed back into the chair. She felt faint, ill.

She took several deep breaths. As much as she didn't want to believe it, everything made sense—Natalie's inquisitiveness, Nick's long work hours, and his business trips that extended into the weekend. *He even had the gall to lie about my health, using me as his excuse for transferring back to the States.* Sam glanced at the stack of unused adhesive notes with Nick in mind—*Keep, Toss, Give Away. What will it be?*

After several minutes pondering her response, Sam opened Nick's briefcase and pulled out the checkbook that bore only his name. Calmly, she wrote out a check for two hundred euros and scribbled her husband's signature. As she addressed the envelope to the Town Hall, her mouth slowly formed into a grin. Yes, she'd return to Detroit. But unlike last time, she wouldn't get angry or sad. She wouldn't even allow depression to attach itself to her. No, the expat assignment in Brussels had indeed been life-changing.

I won't go back to my old life. Neither will Nick. I'll make sure of that. No, we won't slot right back in where we left off—not a snowball's chance in hell.

And with that, Samantha Thomas took great pleasure in signing Nick's name to a second check cleaning out the account.

Marguerite and the Grand Sablon

"Nothing today, I'm afraid, Madame Vogel. That pattern you're after is quite rare. Grandfather and I will keep looking."

Marguerite Vogel shrugged, offering a stoic face to Gaspard Renard. The well-dressed young man was a dealer in fine china, silver, and other curiosities. He and his grandfather were regulars at the antique market whose red tents and green awnings sprouted up each weekend in front of the magnificent Church of Our Blessed Lady of the Sablon.

The Grand Sablon was one of the city's most chic neighborhoods. Cafés, restaurants, boutiques, galleries, and that most ubiquitous of Brussels' offerings, chocolate shops, ringed the rectangular square. The narrow streets winding away from the Grand Sablon were among the city's oldest. They housed even more art galleries and antique shops. The latter were of particular interest to Marguerite.

Of all the vendors with whom Marguerite dealt, the firm of Renard and Renard was her favorite. They offered wares at fair prices. The elder Renard, a dapper gentleman about Marguerite's age, frequently extended discounts to her simply because *she had a lovely smile*.

"Looking for number five, isn't that right?"

Marguerite adjusted the knot of the red headscarf that covered all but the bangs of her gray hair. "Number six." The pride in the old woman's voice was unmistakable. "Found a complete setting at Marolles, of all places." She wanted to add that she snared the fine

Belgian china for a fraction of what she'd have to pay a Grand Sablon dealer like Renard, but she didn't want to offend the man. She needed the help of every one of her contacts in the antique trade to complete her quest. And time was running out. "Regards to your grandfather. Good day, Gaspard."

Marguerite was disappointed. She'd combed the entire market and, with the exception of a butter knife, found nothing on her wish list. Her mind raced through the inventory of remaining items, causing her great agitation. She pulled the purple tweed coat tightly around her torso and lifted her chin, muttering aloud as was her custom. "A café Russe and Wittamer pastry will cheer me up."

She was about to emerge from under the market's green awnings when out of the corner of her eye she caught a flash of red. *The exact shade of crimson,* she thought. Hugging her shopping bag to her coat, she hobbled through the crowd of shoppers with determination. Her cane, handcrafted from silver and ebony, nudged those in her path.

A burly couple in matching green hunter jackets, however, blocked Marguerite's access to the stall. *Germans,* she inferred upon hearing them banter back and forth. "How much cost…the ret *tafel* cloth?" the blonde woman asked the dealer in broken English.

Marguerite had to act fast. "Oh, oh, oh," she moaned, clutching her chest. But her effort failed. To get their attention, she elbowed the German man in the back before reprising her chest-clutching pantomime.

The couple turned, concern flashing on their round, robust faces. "Are you all right?" the tall woman asked.

Marguerite used the opportunity to push between the couple. She clutched the stall's table of wares for effect. "Fine, fine. All fine now. Just a little spell. Get them every now and then." She inhaled deeply, exaggerating a wheezing sound.

The man's hand hovered near Marguerite as if worried she might fall. "Do you *vish* to sit?" He pointed to a nineteenth-century settee for sale in the adjoining stall.

Taking little sips of air, Marguerite shook her head. "I'm okay. Just never know…when it may…hit again. One time I came to, found myself flat on my back." She motioned to the asphalt parking lot that served as the market's weekend home.

"Terrible," replied the man.

"You poor thing," said the woman.

"Oh, not to worry. Some kind soul always comes to my aid even if it means a trip to the hospital and a police report for the Good Samaritan."

Her scare tactics worked like a charm. The German couple exchanged looks and backed away. She watched them sidle up to a nearby stall that sold books and ancient maps. Turning, Marguerite met the raised eyebrows and scowl of the stall's heavily wrinkled owner.

"Good day, Madame Vogel."

She knew that Madame Martens wouldn't be too cross with her for shooing away potential customers. Marguerite was one of her most loyal patrons. Over the past decade she'd already bought several items from the raspy-voiced dealer, including eight linen napkins, five silver napkin rings, and a silk buffet runner, all at outrageous prices. Madame Martens could count on Marguerite's deep pockets for more sales if she brought additional items on her wish list to market.

Madame Martens stood with her arms across her chest. "So you're interested in the red tablecloth?" Her smug tone suggested something more, the whiff of opportunity.

Marguerite glared at her. *You know I am, you old cow. It's exactly what I've been looking for. A perfect match for the runner you sold me five years ago.*

Marguerite assumed a sugary smile. "Maybe yes, maybe no. I'll take a closer look. Frankly, Madame, if you were so certain of my interest, I'd have thought you'd put it aside for me. Your commercial instincts are usually so…*admirable,* shall we say."

"You can't expect me to remember all of my customers' special orders." Madame Martens tugged the antique French tablecloth from the middle of the fabric pile. She laid it out, smoothing the fine linen with her hands.

Marguerite pinched the fabric between her thumb and forefinger. Removing her spectacles, she bent over the table to better inspect the pattern and weave.

"Well?"

Ignoring the woman, Marguerite flipped over an edge of the fabric. "Might work," she mumbled to herself. The rich red tones were a match, as was the jacquard chrysanthemum pattern. But the cloth's dimensions and unique six-inch border of gold silk made it the perfect table linen, a veritable coup toward completing her mission. "Yes," she added with a decisive nod of her head. "This will work very nicely."

Madame Martens cleared her throat. "Now that you mention it, I see that it's a perfect match for the buffet runner I sold you some years back. Ideal complement for the napkins you bought as well. You simply must take it. Foolish not to."

"Maybe, maybe not," Marguerite said. She began to finger through the pile of fabric, pulling out a different cloth, more orange than red. "How much for this one?"

Madame Martens scoffed. "You don't want that tablecloth. Practically said so yourself."

Marguerite looked up with a guilty grin. She knew she was a terrible negotiator. Her unfiltered ramblings didn't help matters either. She could never match the skills of her late husband Charlie. Not only could he persuade any shopkeeper to accept a lower price, Charlie was so good at sweet-talking, the merchant shook hands to the deal, believing the steep discount was his own idea.

"Very well then. How much?"

Madame Martens' customary scowl surrendered to a wide smile. "It's vintage fabric. French. Border's authentic silk. Pristine condition as you can see."

Marguerite seethed on the inside but kept her composure. The date of her planned celebration was fast approaching. With so many pieces to go, she couldn't afford to pass on something as important as the tablecloth.

"If you don't take it," the cloth dealer added, "I'm sure that nice German couple—"

Marguerite fixed her sparkling blue eyes on the woman. "Madame Martens, I don't expect you to give me the tablecloth for free. I'm prepared to deal with you fairly, but I'm almost ninety. I do need to know the price before I drop dead."

Turning red, Madame Martens twisted herself upright until she stood as rigid as a broomstick. "Well," she huffed, "I was simply trying to point out the high quality of the tablecloth. Let me think. It's fo…, no fi…, I mean…six, *six* hundred euros."

Marguerite took a deep breath. That was much more than she expected to pay—more than the cloth was worth. But she had no choice. It was futile to barter with the woman who sensed a buyer's desire with the instincts of a shark. She leaned over her purse, fingers fumbling through her wallet for the bundle of euros when she suddenly heard Madame Martens bellow, "How dare you!"

Marguerite looked up, her mouth open. "W…what? I…I didn't do—"

Madame Martens' nicotine-stained finger pointed over Marguerite's shoulder. "Not you, *him*."

Marguerite turned to find the elder Monsieur Renard. His cherubic face, crinkly eyes, and wispy white hair always brought a smile to her face.

He tipped his large bowler hat toward Marguerite. "Good day, Madame Vogel. Seems Madame Martens doesn't appreciate my—"

"Sticking your nose, judgmental sneer, and disapproving head shake into my affairs. I don't meddle in your business, Monsieur Renard, and I'd—"

"But you gladly accept my referrals. Five in the last three weeks alone."

Madame Martens stammered, "W…well y…yes, I do. Merely one of the ways we dealers help each other."

He stood firmer, widening his stance. The sharp creases of his black trousers rested on top of the polished dress shoes. "And in that spirit of camaraderie, I was offering my assistance now."

Madame Martens leaned across her table of stacked linens. "How? By interfering with a sale."

"By helping you stay competitive. I happen to know that a cloth very similar if not the very twin of this one," he said, gesturing toward the red table linen, "can he bought around the corner for two hundred euros."

Taking the man's sly wink as her cue, Marguerite pulled out three crisp bills and waved them in Madame Martens' face. "I'm willing to pay three."

With the prized tablecloth tucked away into her shopping bag, Marguerite made her way back to her savior's stall. She found the elder Renard discussing the day's receipts with his grandson when she interrupted them. "*Merci, merci,* Monsieur Renard. How can I ever thank you?"

The old gentleman smoothed his red tie before accepting her hand. "Just keep gracing Renard and Renard with that lovely smile."

Marguerite felt her cheeks warm. "You're too kind. I was thinking of something more tangible. How about coffee and pastry to celebrate my good find? My treat, of course."

Marguerite and Monsieur Renard left the market. But instead of veering toward the café's large pink awning, Marguerite guided her escort across the street to a designer boutique.

"Don't tell me you're interested in buying shoes—*those* shoes anyway."

Marguerite snickered. "Of course not. I'm nearly ninety. Couldn't walk three steps in those heels. But they're so outrageous I adore them." She stopped before the shop's colorful window display. "No harm looking."

Marguerite had no idea what the shoes cost, but based upon the store's clientele she knew they had to be very dear. Customers were not mere browsers who simply popped into the shop for a look-see, but veritable shoppers who popped out again with a purchase.

She lifted her foot and twirled a black leather orthopedic shoe with a thick rubber sole. "If only these monstrosities came with sequins, jewels, and blood-red soles."

A female spoke from behind. "You might be onto something, Madame Vogel. A new line perhaps?"

Marguerite and Monsieur Renard both turned toward the sweet, youthful voice.

"Why, if it isn't darling Charlotte," Marguerite said before leaning in to kiss the cheeks of the plainly dressed young woman. "How are you, my dear?"

"All good. Just popped out for lunch."

Marguerite introduced her two acquaintances. She explained that Charlotte worked as a sales clerk in the designer shoe store. "We both have a sweet tooth for pastry." Marguerite added that she and the young woman had met sharing a table at Wittamer Café one busy Saturday.

"Friends ever since," Charlotte said with a wink. "She even gave me this." The young woman pulled out a scarlet red scarf from under her gray raincoat.

"Lovely, very lovely," Monsieur Renard said before nodding to Charlotte's feet. "If you don't mind my asking, dear girl, why don't you wear those fancy shoes you sell?"

Marguerite and Charlotte exchanged a look and shared a giggle. Marguerite confessed that she had asked the young woman that very question on their first meeting.

"They're just not me. Father says I'm very sensible. Says I should dress as such." With that, she tucked the bright red scarf back under her raincoat.

From their prior conversations, Marguerite knew that Charlotte lived at home. She didn't have a young man, something about a promise made to her late mother about looking after her father whose paternal counsel extended to his daughter's hairstyle, makeup, and friends. Charlotte, Marguerite believed, was a sparkling gem whose luster dulled under layers of practicality.

"By the way, Marguerite, got a lead for you." Charlotte explained that a woman who came into the shop had mentioned that she owned an antique store in Namur that specialized in china. "Well, you know I just had to ask," Charlotte added, her big brown eyes dancing with excitement. "I described the pattern you're after. And what do you know? She thinks she can put her hands on a complete place setting. Maybe two." Charlotte fished inside her handbag and handed the woman's business card to Marguerite.

Marguerite's spirit soared with delight. "You are a dear, dear girl. I knew there was a reason fate threw us together."

Marguerite's frequent excursions into the Grand Sablon made her something of a local celebrity. After being interrupted by several other people who hurried out of the square's shops to greet her, Marguerite and Monsieur Renard finally reached the café, grabbing an outside table under its expansive awning. They both ordered coffee, but Monsieur Renard declined the pastry. His gaze wandered toward the shoe shop. "Charlotte is exactly the kind of young woman I wish Gaspard would find. Pretty and practical. Good head on those shoulders."

Marguerite lifted a napkin to dab the corners of her mouth. "It's always pained me to see your grandson without a partner. He's so handsome and charming. I simply figured he hadn't met the right young woman…or *man*."

Monsieur Renard's eyes widened. "No, no, no. Gaspard's not like that."

"Has he told you?"

"No."

"Then how would you know?"

"I'd know."

"And if he were, what—"

"But he's not."

Marguerite patted Monsieur Renard's arm. "What would it matter? That's all I'm saying. You want him to be happy, no? We don't choose those we love, Monsieur."

A glint in his eye told Marguerite she'd hit her mark. Monsieur Renard nodded slowly. "Perhaps you're right. The boy's grandmother and I were a most unlikely match. Mathilde's parents were killed in the war. Her grandmother, old banking money, didn't think much of a struggling antique dealer. I was only good enough for the service door. 'Keep the peddler out of the parlor,' I heard the old woman call down the stairs often enough." A distant image seemed to spark a wistful smile. "Love of my life, Mathilde was. Her green eyes always looked at me as if I were her prince."

Marguerite guessed that he was too proud or maybe embarrassed to draw attention to the tears welling in his eyes. She plucked the silk handkerchief from the pocket of his suit coat and dabbed his eyes.

Monsieur Renard took her hand and held it to his lips. "Thank you, dear woman. And you, Marguerite, did the course of true love run smooth?"

"Of course not, you silly fool. Does it ever?"

After licking whipped cream from her lips, Marguerite described her courtship. Her mother was furious with her own younger sister, Marguerite's godmother and namesake, for inviting Karl Vogel to a dinner party. Margot, as her aunt liked to be called, seated the dashing artist directly across the table from her young and impressionable niece. "Aunt Margot was a free spirit. A poet, fashion designer, and self-proclaimed bohemian. She hosted soirées for the most interesting people in Brussels. Mother called her a crazy old maid, but I saw only a brilliant personality."

Marguerite's parents weren't keen on Karl, especially as their daughter's suitor. "He was twelve years older than me—and German.

Fought in the war…on the wrong side. Today, of course, it doesn't matter, but seventy years ago, scars were still fresh. I was nineteen and madly in love. The night we met was magical."

"And you stayed happy?"

Marguerite sighed. "I fell in love with Charlie over and over again, nearly every day of our marriage. Until the tragedy, of course…"

Before Monsieur Renard could respond, a second whipped-cream cake appeared on the table. He gazed up at the server. "We didn't order—"

Marguerite's energetic outburst interrupted him. "Dear Giovanni. I didn't see you."

"They had me hidden inside. But when I spotted you on the terrace, I simply had to bring out your favorite pastry. On the house."

Marguerite introduced the handsome Italian to Monsieur Renard. She'd befriended the friendly waiter on her all-too-frequent outings to the café for a café Russe and pastry. Giovanni worked constantly, saving money to open a restaurant of his own.

The energetic waiter pulled a handwritten note from a pocket of his trousers. "Before I forget, here's contact information for my uncle Roberto. He specializes in silver and glassware. Says he can find anything you need. He lives in Milan but travels to Belgium all the time."

"*Grazie, grazie mille,* dear boy," Marguerite said, putting the paper into her purse.

After Giovanni said goodbye, Monsieur Renard spoke. "Dear woman, is there no one in the entire Grand Sablon unaware of your mysterious quest?"

―――∘((•))∘―――

Marguerite's aunt had done more for her niece than merely introduce her to Karl "Charlie" Vogel. Upon her death, Aunt Margot left her niece the tall, narrow house on Rue aux Laines. Marguerite and Charlie lived together in the house for more than forty-five years. They were happy, too busy with life and too much in love to have children.

"Anniversaries and birthdays don't wait for anyone." Marguerite spoke those words to herself every morning for motivation to rise out of bed and venture into the gloomy and chilly winter air. She wasn't maudlin about death. She faced it with a survivor's perspective. Almost ninety, she'd outlived most of her contemporaries. Those very close to her, including her husband, had died. The approaching decade, she knew, would likely be her last. But she wasn't bitter. She'd been given a good, long life. More importantly, the dream of the special dinner party filled her with purpose.

Over the next few months, Marguerite acquired much of the missing china and table decoration. Giovanni's uncle was able to supply the remaining pieces of silverware, including the serving utensils. In addition, a trip to Namur proved fortuitous indeed. Charlotte's contact, the antique dealer, was able to put her hands on one complete place setting as well as several pieces for the seventh and penultimate setting. Marguerite decided she could live without the bread plate, and cup and saucer, but she simply had to find the dinner plate. If successful, that left only the eighth and final setting.

With an eye on the calendar, Marguerite had put the Renards and all the other antique dealers on notice. She returned to Marolles, the open-air flea market in Place du Jeu de Balle, almost daily and scoured other shops in and around the Grand Sablon and Rue Haute. Her forays turned up a serving platter and bowl as well as the pieces to complete the seventh setting. But an eighth setting proved elusive.

On a dreary Saturday in January, Marguerite ventured into the antique market. Her mood matched the weather. She browsed several stalls before coming upon that of her good friends. Both Renards were too busy with other customers to notice her.

"My dear Charlie," she said to herself. "It looks hopeless."

"Will you not share with me what you have planned?"

She looked up from the box of china to find the elder Monsieur

Renard. His expression of concern drew her empathy. She felt compelled to share bits of her secret. "I know it sounds silly, probably even crazy. I want the final setting for…Charlie." The surprise on Monsieur Renard's face wasn't unexpected. "Symbolic, of course. It's important to me that Charlie be there…in spirit. A place at the table if you will. But…only a month away."

Monsieur Renard squeezed her arm. "No need to explain, dear woman. I often speak to Mathilde. Let me see what I can do."

Two weeks before the celebration, Marguerite picked up the engraved invitations. Despite her disappointment at not finding an eighth place setting, satisfaction swept over her as she flipped through the envelopes. Embossed in gold were the names of her guests.

Madame Marguerite Vogel kindly requests your presence for dinner
To be held in her home on Rue aux Laines,
on Saturday, February the fourteenth at eight o'clock in the evening.
Guests are requested to bring an open heart and wear something fun!

With secret delight, she tuned into the gossip buzzing about the Grand Sablon. Everyone was curious about the man in formal wear including top hat, tails, and white gloves who stepped out of a vintage Rolls Royce to deliver invitations to select recipients. The man's mission was a mystery to all but Marguerite and her invitees. And even those receiving the fancy invitation could only guess the reason for the dinner party and why they were among the chosen few.

The date of the dinner arrived. Caterers busied themselves in the kitchen, filling the house with the aromas of roasted meats, baked breads, and other delicacies. Marguerite hummed the opening measures of Lehár's "Merry Widow Waltz" as she glided through the dining room in a purple ballroom gown. She'd spent the better part of the afternoon carefully laying out the table, the sight of which filled her with pride and delight. The fine bone china had a delicate floral border of light blue. An art-deco pattern adorned the meticulously polished silver. Lead crystal shimmered with a pink hue under a Venetian chandelier.

"You've done it, Marguerite," she said, before glancing at the single empty space at the table. "Well, almost. But it'll have to do, right, my dear, sweet Charlie?"

She looked down at her feet and giggled. A week before, as a means of accepting Marguerite's invitation, Charlotte had sent along a pair of orthopedic shoes bedazzled with sequins and rhinestones. But it was the shoes' red soles that made Marguerite most giddy.

Marguerite looked around at the empty places, imagining the many wonderful people with whom she and Charlie had shared the table for nearly fifty years. She moved to the middle of the room and held onto the back of a chair, its freshly polished mahogany smooth to the touch. As she gazed across the table, her mind traveled back exactly seventy years to the very night she first set eyes on the dashing Karl Vogel.

But every recollection of the couple's first meeting stirred a second memory, haunting images of the tragedy that separated them forever. It was twenty years ago. The couple prepared to celebrate the fiftieth anniversary of their first meeting. Marguerite was in the Grand Sablon, making final arrangements for that night's dinner party. A fire broke out in a neighboring house. It spread quickly. Charlie was in his attic studio, painting. Trapped, he died of smoke inhalation. The blaze spared much of the house and Marguerite's prized possessions including many of Charlie's and her aunt's paintings and sculptures. But in a painful stroke of irony, the room that sustained the heaviest damage was the dining room, its table fully set for that evening's golden anniversary celebration.

Friends advised her to move—*too many memories*. But Marguerite refused. "Memories are all I have left of Charlie. Most of those—the happiest, in fact—were made in this house."

The structure and furnishings were easily replaced. But Marguerite felt cheated, robbed of Charlie and a full measure of happiness. Bitter, she withdrew from the world, living as a recluse. Ten years after the fire, on what would have been the couple's sixtieth anniversary of meeting, an idea came to her. She'd restore the dining room to its former grandeur and recreate the meal served the night she and Charlie met. It would be the very same celebration she'd planned for their fiftieth anniversary. With her friends dying off, she had a dilemma. But a happy solution soon dawned on her. She'd fill her table with people like Charlie and herself. *Dear souls who deserve a chance at true love.*

Though sometimes worried that the quest was foolish, Marguerite drew comfort knowing that it gave her purpose, a reason to mingle among the living. After a decade of searching, and with the aid of many friends like Charlotte, Giovanni, the Renards, and many others, she'd nearly completed her mission.

"I know you're all wondering why I brought you here. Well, tonight marks—"

The sound of the door buzzer interrupted Marguerite's toast. As those seated in the opulent dining room waited for Giovanni to return from answering the door, they spoke of music, art, and poetry. Marguerite thought how proud Aunt Margot would have been. She felt Charlie's presence even though she failed to find a symbolic china setting for his place at the table.

A commotion on the stairs continued in the hall outside the dining room. Monsieur Renard entered first, wearing a long wool overcoat. He held a bowler in his hand. He huffed and puffed, holding his chest as he caught his breath.

"Monsieur Renard," Marguerite cried, rising to her feet. "Is everything okay?"

"Not merely okay, *exceptional*." He looked toward the door as Giovanni reentered the room. The young man, looking dapper in a black dinner jacket, scarlet shirt, and jeans, carried a wooden crate in his arms. "No, not the table, young man," Monsieur Renard said. "There, on the empty chair."

Everyone jumped to their feet and clustered around the crate. Monsieur Renard motioned to his grandson. "Gaspard, will you do us the honor?"

As Gaspard plunged his hand down into the straw, a broad grin swept across his face. He pulled out the first item, a coffee cup. The delicate blue pattern matched the china on the table.

Marguerite gasped. Her hand flew to her cheek. "It isn't?"

Monsieur Renard beamed with pride. "It is. The final place setting." He held out his hands to embrace the hostess who radiated with joy. "Happy birthday, dear Marguerite."

Marguerite blushed. "But it's not my birthday."

The other guests exchanged glances. Whispers suggested surprise at Marguerite's declaration.

Monsieur Renard's arm swept across the table. "But all this? I don't understand. You've been talking for months about your ninetieth birthday. I just assumed."

Nodding heads suggested that others thought the same thing.

Marguerite looked flustered. "Oh my, my, my. I guess I have been going on about my milestone. A bit too self-absorbed, perhaps. But that's not for two months."

Monsieur Renard took her hand. "Then what's the meaning of this dinner?"

Marguerite became more animated. Her blue eyes sparkled in the candlelight. "I was just about to get to that when you interrupted."

She took the plate, handling it with great care and placing it before the empty chair. Others brought crystal stemware, linen, and silver from the sideboard. Marguerite filled the wineglass and motioned Monsieur Renard to the chair. "Please."

He shook his head. "I couldn't. Isn't this the place reserved for your late husband?"

Marguerite kissed his cheek. "I was wrong, foolish. Almost repeated the mistake that kept me locked away for ten years." She gazed around the room. "Look at these young faces. This house is alive for the first time in decades. Charlie would agree. Antiques—china, silver, old people like me—only gather dust on a shelf." She pulled out the chair. "Please, Monsieur Renard."

As everyone took their seats, all eyes turned to Marguerite for her toast and, more importantly, her explanation.

Marguerite hoisted her glass. "Seventy years ago, tonight, in this very room, I set eyes upon the man who became the love of my life. I didn't care what anyone thought…age, nationality, profession. None of that mattered. When we looked into each other's eyes…" She heaved a heavy sigh.

"Here, here," someone yelled. Glasses clanked and everyone drank.

Marguerite fought back a tear. "Wait, let me finish. We're not here simply to honor the past. Each of you is very special to me. You helped make this evening possible. Even more, you gave this ancient woman friendship and purpose. I want to give something back."

By this time, all eyes had begun to tear. Again Marguerite lifted her glass, prompting others to do the same. "May each of your lovely hearts open tonight to endless possibilities."

As they drank from rose-hued crystal goblets, Marguerite studied her dinner guests. The Grand Sablon connected them all. Charlotte emerged from her drab shell. The young shop clerk looked radiant in a red dress accessorized with a wild pair of the designer shoes she sold. She sat across from the sharp young Dutchman who owned a promising new art gallery. He had found the Italian vase that served as the table's centerpiece. Giovanni was seated across from a striking woman from Ghent, a poet and baker of designer cakes. She had researched recipes to Marguerite's exact specifications, recreating the rich chocolate torte first served up seventy years earlier. Lastly, there were Monsieur Renard's handsome grandson and a dashing French wine merchant. Gaspard Renard had traded his conservative wools for a silk peacock-blue dinner jacket. Marguerite had found the perfect suitor for him. The witty Frenchman owned a trendy wine bar in the cellar of a building just off the Grand Sablon. At Marguerite's instruction, he had secured several bottles of vintage wine for the evening.

In her search for the china service, Marguerite had befriended a wonderful assortment of local characters. She had pieced together an evening of promise and hope with some of the kindest and loneliest spirits in the Grand Sablon. She couldn't force love to blossom for her new friends, but she hoped to nudge things along with a little help from Charlie and a healthy dose of old-fashioned romance.

Marguerite glanced over the arrangement of red and pink roses, violets, and forget-me-nots, a perfect match of the flowers that had graced the table seventy years before. Her heart lifted at the sight of a beaming Monsieur Renard who raised his glass. "To Marguerite, the loveliest lady of the Grand Sablon."

Acknowledgments

I extend my deepest gratitude to:

My husband Jim. His hard work and tenacity made our Brussels adventure possible. His love and encouragement are limitless. Despite a demanding job, he always makes time to read every word I write.

The Brussels Writers Circle. This dedicated and skilled collection of writers was a source of camaraderie and inspiration. Welcoming Jim and me into their circle, they extended their friendship. They provided inspirational sustenance to weather many a dark and gloomy night, and deflated spirit.

The Barrington Writers Workshop. This talented group, my first circle of writers, saw me off on my Brussels adventure and welcomed me back again into their fold. Their respectful and insightful critiques help make me a better writer.

Editor, Meera Dash. She combed the manuscript with great care, keeping my readers from poor grammar, sloppy text, and careless commas. Her keen eye saved me from eternal embarrassment.

Susan Jackson O'Leary. She came to my rescue with her creative eye to produce the book's cover art.

Friends Barbara, Gia, MaryEllen, Lorna, Peg, Kathrin, and Charlie. Readers of early drafts, they helped me shape and polish the final stories with valuable insights. Their support and encouragement are treasured.

Karina and her friendly staff at Bocca Moka, our favorite café in Brussels. I spent countless hours over flat whites and café lungo crafting stories and observing life in our adopted city.

Barbara, our Brussels neighbor at number 6. This kind woman with a big heart for animals not only extended us her friendship, but also gifted us one of her rescues, recognizing that the impish fellow wanted to adopt us.

Sadie, our golden retriever, and Puhi, our Belgian "guest cat." Their furry company and unconditional love soothed many bouts of writer's stress.